THE MORE THE MERRIER

A Dark Christmas Novella

SYBIL KNIGHT

SK PRYNTZ

SOCIALS:

Sybil Knight:
HTTPS://LINKTR.EE/AUTHORSYBILKNIGHT

SK Pryntz:
HTTP://LINKTREE.COM/SKPRYNTZAUTHOR

DEDICATION:

To those of you who came for the nine dicks in the story but stayed for the two cunts who wrote it.

TRIGGER WARNING:

PLEASE BE ADVISED THAT THIS IS A WORK OF FICTION, AND ACTS PORTRAYED IN THIS BOOK COULD LEAD TO DISFIGUREMENT AND/OR SEVERE INJURY. ACTS PORTRAYED IN THIS BOOK **SHOULD NOT** BE ATTEMPTED IN REAL LIFE.

ADDITIONALLY, THE AUTHORS ASK THAT YOU HEED THE FOLLOWING LIST OF POTENTIAL TRIGGERS:

- OVERALL SEXUALLY EXPLICIT AND VIOLENT CONTENT
- FORCED DRUGGING
- WEED (SO MUCH WEED)
- DEATH AND MURDER
- PTSD AND TRAUMA
- GRAPHIC INJURIES
- MENTIONS OF DRUG USE/ ABUSE
- ALCOHOL USE AND ABUSE
- SEX ADDICTION
- DP

- SOMNO
- DEGRADATION AND HUMILIATION AND PISS PLAY
- VOYEURISM
- SWORD CROSSING (LOTS AND LOTS OF SWORD CROSSING
- NONCON/DUBCON
- MENTAL HEALTH REP
- TWINCEST (HER WITH THEM)
- REINDEER GAMES AKA PRIMAL PLAY WITH DEER SKULLS
- CHRISTMAS LIGHTS UP THE BUM
- BONDAGE
- FORCED EJACULATION
- SUGGESTED ACCIDENTAL NECRO AND DESECRATION OF A CORPSE
- SEXUAL COERCION
- ORGIES
- INAPPROPRIATE USE OF BINGO MARKERS
- AND MORE...

PROLOGUE
NICKIE

Don't look. Don't look. Don't look. Don't you dare look,
ya dumb twat.

I could hear sissy's voice yelling at me in my
head. Instead of chancing a glance behind me like that
little defiant streak wanted me to do—I hated being
bossed around just because someone was a bit older or
bigger—I stared up at the night sky and then down at the
blood coating my hands. It was still sticky and wet to the
touch. Warm too. But I didn't have time to think about
where it all came from when I needed to be running.

I had to keep running or they'd find me and they'd...

I shook those thoughts away and lifted my knees as
high as they would go while my shoes struggled to cut
through all the freshly fallen snow. My ass wasn't made for
this weather. The sudden gust of wind that billowed out
my t-shirt, shot straight through my leggings, and traveled
up my spine like a creepy-crawly spider reminded me that
these clothes weren't neither.

That's what ya get for being vain, Nickie.

Noelle piped up again, and I refused to prove her right. To prove any of them right. I wasn't a brat just because I didn't like to share my things. They were mine. There weren't nothin' wrong with that.

I swiped at my face, at the tiny popsicle tears forming on my cheeks every time I sucked in a breath, and a puff of white air danced around in front of me. A little farther. I just had to push myself a little farther.

I could already make out the flickering candlelight in the cabin window. But before I could get there, my foot caught on a fallen branch and I tumbled head over ass the last several feet down the frozen hill. Rolling to a stop against the pieces of wood stacked up by the front door. With a loud *thud*.

I dusted myself off and ducked behind the pile, squeezing my eyes shut as I counted to ten in my head. When I didn't hear nothing other than the occasional night bird out in the distance, I crept out of my hidey hole and made a mad dash for the door. Tugging on it till my face was blue and my arms were like spaghetti noodles.

It didn't budge, so I stepped up to the window, cupped my hands together, and peered inside. Granny was sittin' her plump ass on her favorite rocker, oblivious to the fact *my* cheeks were freezing off through my leggings. I tapped on the glass over and over until she finally looked up and squinted my way. And then she was hobbling towards the door with her knitting needle in hand. She swung it open and stared at me.

"Hey, Gran! You locked me out again!" I smiled at her.

She paused a moment to look me over, but Granny appeared to not be seeing much of anything these days.

"I'm sorry, dear. Come on in. Let's warm you up."

CHAPTER 1
NICKIE

"**B**ingo!" I pulled the box out from under the bed and peeked inside at the contents.

Looks like Granny knows how to have a little fun after all. It wasn't necessarily the good shit, but who was I to complain about free weed?

Old people were notorious for leaving lighters around, so it didn't take me long to find one in the junk drawer in the kitchen. I relaxed as soon as I took that first hit.

The cookies in the oven were making everything reek like potpourri, but it gave the room a better smell than the stink she had perforating the walls. Nothing was worse than old people stink.

"Holy fuck, Gran, this place smells like rotten eggs. Not sure the cookies are gonna be enough."

Granny wasn't gonna respond, obviously, but talking to myself felt better than admitting I was alone.

Why did I think it was a good idea to come here again?

The radio crackled as the song ended, and I turned the dial until another one came through. This one was something twinkly and festive like Granny's personality. It was the kind that made everything seem so... *happy.*

I swayed to the rhythm as I cleaned up the counter, wiping away the crumbs and tossing out the plastic wrap while humming Christmas carols under my breath. The air was thick with a mixture of sugar, cinnamon, and Granny's stash. My cheeks were warm, and my apron—calling me *the best chef alive*—was dusted with white powder. I kept telling Granny this shit would kill her one day, but that old bat didn't listen for shit.

"Almost Christmas, Gran," I said in a cheery, sing-song voice while dancing around the pine needles littering the floor.

In the corner, where Granny's old rocker sat, a crooked pine tree leaned against the wall, still spitting its pokey branches onto the hardwood. I'd dragged it in myself this morning. It'd hurt my face to be outside in this cold, but it was worth it, especially after I'd found the perfect little guy rooted behind the house. It was wet with frost and still smelled like the forest. It wasn't pretty—not exactly like the ones in magazines. Hell, half the branches were bare, and one side was so flat it looked like it had been crushed beneath a car tire.

But it was mine. *Ours.*

I smiled. "We'll fix you, wittle tree, won't we? Granny loves Christmas."

The lights I'd found in a dusty box in the basement flickered when I plugged them in, glowing weakly like little dying fireflies. I wound them around the tree anyway, humming along to the new music playing. A few of the bulbs had burst, leaving sharp little mouths of glass along the wire, but it added character. I had that too, or so I'd been told more than once over the years.

I cut my finger on one of the edges and stared at the red bead forming on the tip as it dripped down and disappeared into the cracks of the wood below me.

"Well," I said. "A little color never hurt no one, now did it?"

I wiped my hand on my apron and went back to decorating. The ornaments were mismatched, some old and chipped, others handmade by Granny and the little feet that touched these floors long ago. There was a string of popcorn garland, stiff and yellowed with time, but I hung it up anyway. Then, near the top, I tied a bow from Granny's shawl, the crocheted perfection she'd almost finished. It looked beautiful, even with the dark stains at the ends.

"Gran, you'd be so proud," I whispered lovingly. "What d'ya think?"

The rocking chair in the corner seemed to sway for a minute, and I smiled.

I carried the plate of cookies over to the table by the window and set them down beside a single chipped teacup. It was my favorite and reminded me of the cartoon movie we used to watch together. The snow outside had started up again, soft and steady, covering the woods in silence. I pressed a palm against the cold glass, blowing hot air onto the surface and smiling at my reflection. My cheeks were rosy, flour dusted my strawberry hair, and my green eyes were too wide and too bright.

I must have been tired.

"See?" I told Gran softly. "Everything's perfect. Everything's the way you wanted it to be."

The radio fizzled out. It was just the sound of the wind now, and the slow tick of the old cuckoo clock on the back wall.

Then a blurred image in the frosted window moved.

I blinked, leaning closer to the sill. At first, I thought it was just my reflection again, a trick of the eyes. But then it shifted and a shadow outside got close enough to press its hand against mine through the glass. Someone was standing just beyond the light. I could barely make out the outline, but it was tall.

They're watching me.

The smile froze on my lips. I didn't move. I couldn't breathe. The warmth from the oven hummed at my back, and the scent of cookies and that damn pine twisted around the cold draft leaking through the windowsill. My fingers curled against the pane until I felt the warmth transfer from the shadow's hand to mine.

It didn't move either. Just kept watching me.

For a long moment, we stayed like that, separated by a thin slice of glass and a breath of frost. Then I smiled again, slow and deliberate like.

"Gran," I whispered, never taking my eyes off the figure outside. "We have company."

CHAPTER 2
RUDY

The cold hit harder once the sun went down. It crawled through my fucking clothes and bit frosted holes at my skin. My breath looked like smoke from a dying engine. It reminded me of the van and I used that to push my feet harder. We'd been running for hours now—mud on our boots and our hearts pounding like the damn hounds behind us.

"Keep fucking low, or your heads will be target practice for the snipers," I muttered, forcing my way through a tangle of branches. "We're close to the cabin."

Que followed tight behind me, his silhouette a steady shadow in the dark. His body heat kept me going. I knew these fuckers were counting on me. Somehow I managed to get myself into being the leader of the gang of bastards.

Right now one bastard in particular was unusually quiet. Que never shut his damn mouth, unless it was around something. So it was odd that he wasn't singing or cracking jokes about his face being so close to my ass.

I'd never admit it, but with everyone spread out and

the sound of the hounds in the distance, I could really use him humming folk tunes. His presence was a weird comfort. Always had been. Probably always would be.

I could hear him breathing behind me, slow and even, even though his knuckles were raw and his jumpsuit was torn from the struggle of getting free from that hellhole.

"You sure Prat said the cabin was this way? I think you're taking us in fucking circles, Rue-Rue," Que said, mindful to keep his voice low. "And as much as I enjoy staring at your fine ass, I'm freezing my fucking nuts off, dude."

I nodded. "Yeah. Cabin near a lake. Follow the smoke. Said the place seemed safe. He never got close enough to check it out. As for being cold, I'm sure you can find a way to warm up." I glanced over a shoulder. "You think I'm stupid for trusting the Bible-thumper?"

Que snorted. "Meh. I trust him not to run his mouth. Don't know about this magical cabin in the woods, though. As for warming up, *your mouth* on my cock would do just fine."

I almost smiled. Almost. The sound of the dogs carried through the woods again, and it wasn't as distant as before. My gut twisted. "Move your ass or they'll feed your dick to those mutts."

Nothing killed Que's libido, but he nodded and we moved faster. Crouched and quiet, following the faint glimmer of moonlight through the trees where the slight blur of smoke led. Somewhere to our left, a twig snapped and both of us froze. Que raised his makeshift weapon, and I lifted a hand to stop him before he ran off and bludgeoned a squirrel. The woods fell silent again, except for the rush of the creek nearby. Maybe a lake.

Nothing else.

Prat, if you lied to us...

We followed a narrow path, our boots slipping on the wet leaves and the air seeming to get even fucking colder. Finally, the trees broke open, and in the center of a little clearing was a cabin. It was a sagging old thing with a stone chimney puffing faint smoke into the night sky. Our beacon of hope. Warm light flickered in the window, and I ducked, snatching Que by the arm and shoving his ass down with me.

"Fucker didn't bother mentioning that someone lived here," I muttered.

"Yeah." Que narrowed his eyes. "Imma kill him."

I swallowed hard, trying to regroup, while glancing around to see if any of the others had made it here yet. "Maybe he never saw anyone coming and going. They could've popped up outta nowhere, I guess... but now we got a problem."

The closer we got, the more wrong it looked. The snow around the perimeter was trampled—like someone had dragged something heavy through it. Except I didn't see any cars. And pine needles were scattered across the porch. I chanced a look into the window, which was half hidden by a curtain, and I could have sworn I saw a shadow.

A woman's shadow, judging by the shape of it.

"Could be a hunting spot?" Que said quietly. "We could snatch their guns."

"I think I saw a woman," I grunted back.

"Chicks can hunt. God, way to be sexist, man."

I ignored Que's rambling and continued to survey the area, growing more anxious by the minute.

We can't kill whoever's in there. They need to let us in willingly. But we have to survive no matter what.

I crouched behind a log, staring at that faint light streaming out from the house. I could smell the smoke from the chimney, sugar, and something else. Something so sweet it smelled off, like a bottle of perfume left out too long. And sour. Which didn't make much sense.

Que rubbed his hands together for warmth, tugging on my sleeve until I looked back at him. Then he was fluttering those boyish lashes at me. "You think she'll like damsels in distress?"

"She won't get a choice if she doesn't," I said. My voice came out calm, steady, dark like it always did when shit went sideways. "Once the rest of the boys get here, we'll all go in together. But you need to be the one to approach her. Use that charm you claim you have. No noise. No panic. We can get food, warmth, and lie low till we figure out what the fuck to do next."

Que shifted beside me, close enough that I could feel his body heat now. He was smiling, his eyes locked on mine with a playfulness swirling inside the deep pools of blue. "It ain't a claim when you can't deny my charm either. Don't lie. You can't tell me no if you wanted to."

I opened my mouth, planning to argue with him, if only to prove a point, but Que had me pushed against the cabin, my back brushing along the frosted glass. His hands rustled with the snaps on my waist, and I lost my ability to tell the fucker anything.

"Let me hear you say no while your cock is in my mouth."

The shadow moved again, drawing my attention to the window, and I watched her silhouette spin and sway like it was dancing. I could hear faint music playing through the whining of the wind. Something cheerful—holiday bullshit.

The cold slapped at my bare skin, and just as I hissed, the heat of his mouth enveloped me. My hand flew up to rest on the window, my mouth falling open and soft moans escaping me as he sucked my cock like the fucking good boy he could be... when he wanted to be anything.

I glanced down and met Que's eyes, his lips tipping into that all-knowing smirk.

"What the hell are you doing? We can't get caught out here like this. We ca—" My words were cut off by my strangled moans.

"Live a little, Rue-Rue. You're so tightly wound. Relax. I got this. The bitch will let us in, but right now, you need to *let go*. Don't go hiding in your head."

Truth was, I couldn't think about anything but how hot his mouth felt. *Holy fucking hell.* It'd been so long since I had felt him like this. Whenever we could slip away during laundry duty or whenever Que paid off a guard—usually with his mouth—to get us some alone time in my cell.

I wasn't going to last long. I turned my face, my breath fogging the window and my eyes barely open. But then I felt a warmth beneath my palm, and I opened my eyes to look through the glass to find a beautiful red-haired woman staring back at me. Her hand hovering above mine.

I opened my mouth with every intention of warning Que, but the way he sucked my cock and kneaded my balls felt too damn good. So instead, I just stared at the woman as my come shot out and coated his smug fucking face.

"Fuck, I missed that." He grinned as he jumped to his feet and peered over my shoulder. "Who do you think is in there? You know what? Doesn't matter. My turn. I don't care if they can hear—"

Que stopped talking suddenly. He could see her now. A pair of pink lips parted into an O-shape, and emerald-green eyes that were staring right at us.

I smiled, unable to stop the euphoric hum in my blood when I spotted the others making their way towards the cabin from the tree line. Seemed our little Peeping Tom was about to get quite the surprise when nine men appeared on her doorstep offering a bit of holiday cheer.

"Guess we're about to find out."

CHAPTER 3
QUE

I ran a hand over my head, pushing my hair off my forehead and swiping up Rudy's leftover come from my face. Fucker was messy. I liked it when he got messy. Meant that stick up his ass had dropped a bit lower and was close to turtling out.

I gave my fingers a quick lick and then leaned my arm high up on the frame as I used my free hand to offer the cabin door a few light raps. The usual smirk tipping up my mouth so that whoever was on the other side got a front-row seat to my biceps, perfect jawline, and bleach-white teeth.

The ladies loved me. The guys loved me more. And I loved me the most. What could I say? Couldn't be this good-looking *and* humble. Had to save some of the attributes for the rest of 'em.

It only took our mystery woman a quick peek through the peephole before she was tugging the door open and peering at me from the other side. Red hair piled on her head, powdered sugar kissing her cheeks, and wide green eyes that might as well be screaming: *the better to eat ya with, my dear.* Or however the nursery rhyme went. Reading bedtime stories wasn't my thing, not when there was much more fun shit I could be doing under the covers.

Point was, I was the Big Bad Wolf and Miss Riding Hood here wouldn't even see me coming.

She continued to stare at me while I could feel everyone else's eyes on my back from where they were watching our interaction by the tree line.

Good thing I thrived under pressure.

"Hey there, Red. Hate to intrude, but my friends and I got stuck out in this storm. Car's dead and none of us got any cell service." I gestured a thumb behind me. "The big guy over there is getting hitched next week and this was supposed to be his last hurrah—beer, paintball, ya know, the works. You got a landline we can use so he can call the missus? Hate to worry the poor girl for no reason."

I grinned, slipping my foot between the door and the jamb before she could slam it closed. Just in case. At the same time, I dropped my arm from the frame, her eyes following each ripple of muscle as I flexed more than necessary.

I reached up and rubbed at the back of my neck when another gust of wind came blistering through and rose the little hairs at my nape. "It's awfully cold out here. Ain't ya gonna invite us in? Pretty please with powdered sugar on top." I swiped up a glob of the white stuff from the tip of her nose and made a show of licking my finger clean.

I must not have done a good enough job of that the first time, because it tasted like candy and come. Which also happened to be my favorite flavor combination.

The girl shook her head and blinked a few times as if

breaking out of a daze. "Sorry, come on in. Do you like fresh-baked cookies? I made way more than I can eat on my own. Granny always did say my eyes were bigger than my stomach," she rambled on while ushering me farther into the little cabin.

I tossed out a thumbs-up, signaling for the guys to follow me. "Ain't *your granny* ever tell you not to open the door for strangers?" I leaned over the wooden island that now separated us from our eager hostess and attempted to snatch a cookie off the cooling rack.

Red swatted my hand aside and narrowed her glare at me. "If I listened to everything Gran had to say, you'd be stuck out in the cold all night, now wouldn't ya?" She then plucked a spatula from the metal bowl in front of her and took a tentative lick—confirming it met her standards, I suppose.

"Touche," I replied before taking her up on her offer as she tipped the spatula in my direction now. I swallowed it whole, from rubber tip to wooden handle, brushing my lips over where her fingers were still clutching it at one end and pulling back again.

I pushed off the counter and tilted my head to watch as her cheeks turned redder than her hair, rolling back on my heels so that the only thing that seemed threatening about me were my *killer* dimples.

She cleared her throat and crossed her arms over her chest. "Also, we ain't got no phone."

"We?" I questioned as Rudy stepped up behind me. I didn't have to look. I could feel him there. Like a big grumpy presence that sent a delicious chill down my spine.

"Me and Granny. This is her place." The girl hummed as she spun around and dropped the dishes into the sink, oblivious to the fact that she had a bunch of escaped convicts standing in her living room. "Name's Nickie, by the way, and you are?" She glanced from face to face, her smile never dropping despite what I knew she saw there.

Scowls and scathing glares—mostly from my Rue-Rue. Who really was just a big ol' teddy bear. I glanced over my shoulder. *Okay, a grizzly bear. Same, same.* Both had claws and teeth. One just used 'em more.

"I'm Que—short for *too fucking cute to be so painfully single*." I reached an arm back and locked it over Rudy's shoulder. "And this here is Broody Rudy, our blushing groom-to-be." Without bothering to look around, I started naming off the rest of our group one by one. "That there is Dash, Dane, Vix—the twins, Con and Don—what was their mother thinking?" I peered over to my right, pressed an imaginary joint to my lips and made a huffing gesture. "Blitz—I'll give ya one guess as to why we call him that—and..." I double-checked the math in my head, coming up short twice over. "Hey, anyone seen Prat?"

CHAPTER 4
RUDY

*P**rat is missing?*

Fuck. No man left behind. That idiot was the one to tell us how to get here. How could he get lost in the snowstorm?

While Que continued to woo the gullible red-haired woman, I walked around the small cabin trying to get my bearings. There was that strange smell again, mixed with pine sap wafting off the makeshift tree in the living space, and the sweet desserts on the baking tray. My attention got away from me, though, when my eyes caught on Que with her finger in his mouth, those damn hypnotizing eyes glittering like the shitty ornaments on the twig in front of us.

"Didn't take long at all, did you, Thumper?" I murmured, using the nickname I'd given him after that first time we'd fucked and the fucker just kept going. I ran my hands along Que's back where the woman couldn't see.

"Is Nickie short for something?" he continued, pretending to ignore me while his body did the opposite.

"No, silly. Gran named me. She said it was..."

I tuned out the rest of their mindless chatter before I'd be forced to act like I gave a shit. I had a tendency to keep quiet when there was something to observe. Talking made people let down their guard, and I couldn't afford to do that. Ever. It was better that way.

"So sad about your fiancée. She must be missin' you, handsome?"

Que elbowed my side, and I realized the redhead was speaking to me.

"Uh..."

"He's real shook up about missing... Holly." Que didn't skip a damn beat, and that name smacked me square in the face.

Holly, really? I arched a brow at him, but the fucker wasn't looking at me.

"Oh! I'm so sorry. You'll get back to her real soon, Rudy."

I tried to prevent my teeth from cracking as I nodded mechanically, with Que's guided gesture behind the girl's head.

"So you said..."

This time, when the chatter started up again, I ducked away from the two of them and checked in on the rest of the boys. The twins were off to themselves in a corner. Blitz magically found some weed and was surrounded by a thick cloud of smoke while Vix, Dash, and Dane were shoving their fat faces full of sweet treats. Everyone looked happy for once. It was nice to see. They deserved it. We all did.

But where the fuck is Prat?

I slipped outside to get away from the constant hum of

conversation and welcomed the frigid cold as it sobered me up a bit more. There were too many unanswered questions regarding this woman and her grandma.

Where was the old bag anyway? I still didn't see a car—that would have been too easy. Though there were logs piled up by the door and a little shack that looked like it could house a compact vehicle, but the snow was too thick to make out any tracks. It was so fucking cold I couldn't see much of anything, to be honest.

Didn't matter. I had to find Prat. Maybe he was hiding out in a patch of trees or by the lake to throw off the scent of the dogs.

I tried to make my way over there, but the fucking snow was like a white blanket of fog. I couldn't see my hand in front of me, and the longer I stayed out here, the more lost I felt.

"Fucking hell, Prat. You better get here fast."

Begrudgingly, I stepped backwards, not having a choice in the matter if I didn't want to lose track of the cabin and freeze to death myself. While I waited for Prat to appear, I continued to walk the perimeter of the cabin.

No car. No surrounding homes.

I tugged at the back door, it popped open, and I let myself in. The mudroom was filled with a bunch of old shoes and knitting shit that my own grandma used to fiddle with when she made me stupid scarves I pretended to wear during holidays. A red one draped around a creaky old chair caught my attention, and I picked it up, wrapping it around my neck and breathing in the musty scent.

Then I stepped into an adjacent hallway. Making a beeline for the door straight ahead of me. It was the only one pulled closed, so I grabbed on to the knob and twisted.

Hmm. Locked.

All the training they beat into my head forced me back outside, where I rounded the corner of the cabin and located the window that should have led into that room.

Is the grandma sleeping?

The frost was so thick I couldn't see past the glass. I tried to defrost it with my breath, to no avail.

Snap.

I jerked my head around. Expecting Prat's lonely ass to be wandering my way. Instead, my world spun upside down and my vision changed from the snowy tundra by a cabin to another snow-filled night of my life.

I finally fucking had him. My target lined up in my sights. My gun resting on my shoulder and his naked ass propped up on the rim of the hot tub, with some blonde bimbo bouncing on the fucker's shrimp dick. It had taken us years to track him down and lots of red tape to finally get the okay to take him out.

I adjusted my scope, to ensure that I didn't hit the civilian, steadied my breathing, and waited for the perfect moment.

"Oh, fuck! He can't do this to you, can he, baby girl?" the fucker grunted.

"No! Oh god, you feel amazing."

I rolled my eyes, half feeling bad for whatever moron he was talking about and half feeling like the guy deserved it for having piss-poor taste in women. I waited until she flipped around, the blonde hair no longer blocking my view, and settled myself in to take my shot. Until my glare caught on her face. Fucking Holly's face.

My fucking fiancée was cheating on me with the top mafia crime lord in the country.

I saw red. Complete blind rage. The snow didn't feel cold as it pelted down on my skin any longer, while the frothing bubbles of the hot tub remained my only focus.

Call it in, Rudy. Call it in. This is too close.

My teeth were nearly cracking, the scope shaking as my vision was blurred by angry tears.

"Rudy never could—" she started to say and...

Click. Click. Boom.

Another snap wrenched me back from my memories, so that I was now staring at the redheaded woman with powdered sugar still on her cheeks and lips.

"Where are you off to, Nosy Nancy?"

CHAPTER 5
NICKIE

"Why? You got something to hide?" The guy with the dark eyes crossed his arms and quirked a brow. Rudy, Que said his name was—he didn't look much like a Rudy if you asked me. More like a Butch or Diesel. Something as testosterone-filled as he was.

I'd be lyin' if I said I didn't watch the tightening of his muscles and clenching of his jaw as he did it, though. I'd also be lyin' if I said I wasn't watching him for much longer than he realized. At first, it was to figure out what he was doing outside. After I saw the way his face went blank like he was somewhere else entirely—not even flinching against the cold while I was shivering in my sneakers—it was more out of curiosity.

"Me? 'Course not." I pointed from myself to the grumpy beast of a man in front of me. "But there's nothing wrong with keeping some things between us, now is there?"

I grabbed on to his thumb and tugged until he was

following me away from Granny's window and closer to the back door. He let me 'cause there was no chance in hell I was moving him on my own.

"Yeah? What kind of things?"

"The kind a groom knows better than to tell his bride." I dropped my fingers to the waistband of his onesie thing, and he snatched up my wrist.

My eyes flicked to where his nails were digging into my skin, then back to his face. That distant look was still there but so was something else. Annoyance maybe? Never seen that one before. Not when my hands were in a guy's pants.

I leaned in, cupped a palm against my mouth, and whispered, "I won't tell if you won't?"

I batted my lashes a few times, like I always did when Granny told me there was no dessert before dinner. It didn't take more than a little tearing up before she was sneaking some sweets into my hand and warning me not to tell my mother.

I wasn't a brat. I just didn't like being told *no*.

Rudy eyed me for a moment, the cold finally getting to him and causing the little hairs on his arm to stand on end. But he didn't loosen his grip. "You think I'm the sort of guy to cheat on his fiancée?"

I lifted a single shoulder. "I think all guys are. You tellin' me if I dropped to my knees right now and offered to lick ya like a lollipop, you'd turn me down?"

"I'm telling you if you tried it, you wouldn't be licking shit with a busted lip."

"Now that ain't very nice, Mr. Broody." I feigned shock. Truth was, a little blood never bothered me none. Neither did a little pain.

"Don't call me that," he grunted, and shoved my arm back against my chest. Reaching out and tugging me closer again when my foot slipped and I nearly busted my ass on a patch of ice.

"Aw! So ya do care!" I grinned and jumped up to lock my wrists around his neck and my legs around his waist. His arms shot out at his sides like he was afraid to touch me.

I didn't let go, though. Instead, I clung to him like a human-sized starfish. Squeezing tighter with each step he took towards the door until we were standing back inside the cabin. My hair tumbling free from the rubber band I'd found in one of the drawers in the kitchen, and working its way inside Rudy's mouth when he sucked in an annoyed breath.

He blew it back out again. "One of you assholes wanna get off your asses and lend me a hand?"

"What's wrong, Rue-Rue? Can't handle one itty-bitty girl all on your own?" This came from Que. I recognized his voice as he stepped up behind me, and then he was pulling me free and setting me on my feet again. The rest of the guys were all watching us from where they were sprawled out on Granny's sofas or tucked up into the corners of the room.

"That isn't a girl. She's a succubus or something," Rudy grunted. "She tried seducing me out there."

"A suck-you-what?" called out one of the guys.

"I got something you can suck right here, darlin'," added another.

Que *tsked* his tongue, grabbing me by the hand and twirling me around to face him. "You're barking up the wrong tree, Red." He smirked. "The big guy hasn't been with a woman since his fiancée…" His smile dropped and his glare flicked behind me like he was saying something he shouldn't.

"Since his fiancée what?" I pressed.

Que shook his head, his grin firmly back in place like it had never left to begin with. "Since his fiancée agreed to spend the rest of her life chained to that giant ball of fun."

I narrowed my eyes, my left hand making its way to my mouth as I chewed on the tip of my nail, the polish I'd taken from Granny's vanity nearly gone by now. "How about a man?"

"What?" Rudy hissed from behind me.

I spun around to look him in the eye while gesturing a thumb over a shoulder. "He said you haven't been with *a woman* since your fiancée. Not that you haven't been with anyone, so…"

"So?" Rudy repeated.

"So have you? Been with a man?" I could feel myself practically bouncing on my heels. This was better than any of Granny's tv dramas.

"What? No." Rudy appeared taken aback. But not in the offended kinda way. More like in the *hitting a little too close to home* kinda way.

"I don't believe you," I sang out, as I twirled myself around the living room and back into the kitchen.

Those cookies weren't gonna eat themselves, now were they? I glanced down at the half-empty plate that had been piled high a few moments ago. *Or maybe they would…*

CHAPTER 6
QUE

I'd fucked up.

Like *convincing your best friend to cover up a murder, only to have someone find the body you buried in the woods and have it land you both in prison with a life-sentence* sort of fucked-up. It wouldn't be the first time. Probably not the last either. Someone had to protect the fucker from himself. Or at the very least, try.

I could tell by the look Rudy was giving me—a mix between I'd kicked his puppy and he was about to kick mine—that he wasn't happy with me right now.

My knee twisted inwards at the thought.

Guess some part of me knew I deserved it if he did kick me. I never should have mentioned Holly. But the best lies were always the ones that were closest to the truth. He knew that as well as I did. It was also the only excuse I could come up with on short notice. One that made it sound like the rest of us were available, and *he* wasn't.

The big guy had trust issues. Not that I could blame

him. I would have 'em too if I were him. Lucky for everyone, I wasn't him and could think quick on my toes. Apparently not quick enough though, seeing as Red was climbing him like a Christmas tree the moment she'd gotten him alone.

That wasn't my fault. *I mean, how was I supposed to know she would take it as a challenge?*

It didn't matter. This cabin, this girl, none of it was long term. We just needed Prat to get his ass back here and wait for the storm to pass, and we'd all be on our merry way again. Until then, Grumpy-Pants just needed to keep the peace with our fiery little hostess.

Was the girl a tad off the walls? Sure, but there wasn't one of us here who wasn't.

"You and me, talk later," Rudy mumbled under his breath at me, snatching a cookie out of Dash's hand when he wasn't looking.

"Hey!" Dash started to protest. Rudy shot him another glare, and Dash zipped his lips.

I sent Rudy back a mock salute before sidling up next to Nickie, her cheeks puffed out to twice their size and her fingers covered in sugar. She peered over at me through her lashes as she licked 'em clean, one at a time. Ensuring she didn't miss any of the nooks and crannies.

I grinned, swiping my thumb over the empty plate and dusting it across the crotch of my jumpsuit. "Oh, would ya look at that? You missed one."

"Did I?" she hummed.

"You did." I laid a hand on the top of her head and slowly pressed down until she was on her knees, a sea of red cascading over her back and kissing the floor as she repositioned herself in front of me.

I didn't have to say anything else before her fingers were snapping my jumpsuit open and tugging it—*and my underwear*—along my thighs, my cock popping free and bouncing between us. I swiped up more sugar, drawing rings around the girth from base to tip until it resembled a cock-shaped candy cane.

"Merry-fucking-Christmas," I mumbled to myself while one of the twins started chanting, "Jingle bells, Rudy smells, Que's about to get laid!"

"What the fuck are you doing?" Rudy grunted from somewhere behind me, the scraping of chairs against the floor telling me a few of the guys were saddling down and watching. Which was fine with me. My ass enjoyed an audience. My cock did too.

I offered him a thumbs-up and a groan when Nickie bent forward to run her tongue along that large vein at the bottom. "What best men are supposed to do, taking one for the team, Rue-Rue."

Whatever he grumbled in reply was covered up by a wet, slurping sound as Nickie took me all the way back into her throat. Her head bobbing up and down and her tongue twisting 'round and 'round.

Maybe Rudy was right. Maybe this chick was a succubus because it sure as hell felt like she was trying to suck my soul from my body.

I reached out a hand, attempting to grab on to a wall or the counter and nearly tripping on the clothes bunched up around my ankles when she hollowed out her cheeks at the same time she crept an arm behind me and stuck a finger up my ass.

All I could find was the top of a chair, so I held on to that for dear life and made that sound low in my throat, the one I usually made when Rudy was pounding me from behind. My cheeks clenched and my knees buckled, while this girl continued to choke me down and spit me back up as though I was one of those little Vienna sausages you pulled out of a can.

I wasn't. And I'd pull out a ruler to prove it as soon as I could feel my legs again.

"Oh fuck, oh fuck, oh fuck," I hissed out, grabbing the back of Nickie's head and quickly coming down her throat in spirts. She slurped that up just as easily.

When I turned back around, Don and Con were sitting on the couches with their cocks fisted, Blitz was in the corner with a hand shoved down his pants, and Rudy was nowhere to be found.

"Fuck." I pulled my jumpsuit over my ass and tied the sleeves around my waist. It wasn't that Rudy couldn't look out for himself. He was better equipped at that than most people. It was that he didn't care to do it when he was all up in his head. He was also worried about Prat. I could see it in his eyes.

No man left behind, I repeated his stupid mantra. Even if that meant risking his own neck to do it.

"Hey, Tweedle Dick and Tweedle Dim," I yelled out to the twins while making my way towards the back of the house. This cabin wasn't all that big. There were only so many places our fearless leader could be hiding. "Do me a favor and take care of Red."

CHAPTER 7
NICKIE

I kept some of Que's come inside my mouth, swishing it from side to side and back and forth as I watched the twins rise from their chairs and stalk towards me. These boys were fucking delicious. Better than the cookie recipe I'd found on Granny's nightstand and twice as nice as the pot I'd sprinkled on top of the batter and mixed around until you couldn't see the little flakes anymore.

I could hear Noelle's voice in my head again before it twisted and twirled into Granny's.

Now, now, Nickie, dear. Leave something to the imagination. Don't give it to those boys so easy. No one likes a floozy.

Yeah, yeah, Gran. Eat a dick.

Or maybe I should eat it for her? I looked the twins over and grinned like the cat that was just about to suck off the canary.

"Hear that, Don? We need to take care of the *little toy* Que left for us," one of them said.

The other nodded and licked his lips. "Yeah, Con. How ever can we entertain her?"

I smiled, pulling off my shirt and watching how everyone's eyes stayed glued on me. I might not have liked sharing with my sister but these boys didn't seem to mind it all that much. And I didn't mind it neither.

The guy in the corner gave me a longing stare. Then he flicked his joint to the side and gripped his cock with both hands.

"I can think of a few ways, boys." I shrugged a shoulder and jumped up on one of the counter stools, spreading my legs wide for them. Wide enough for two of 'em if they didn't mind a little brotherly competition.

"Mmm. You are one hell of a naughty thing, aren't you?" they asked in almost perfect unison.

I moaned in response, slipping a hand into the waistband of my leggings and splashing my fingers around in the wetness I found there. "*Come* find out?"

The twins all but raced forward, and Con—or was it Don? Well, whichever one it was, he gripped his cock while the other got down on his knees in front of me and dragged my leggings along my thighs before lowering his head to my clit. His brother squeezed in beside him so that the lookalikes were shoulder to shoulder. Jerking each other off while they alternated between eating me out.

"So fun to play with. Scream for us like the *little toy* you are," the twin on the left whispered against my pussy lips before diving in nose first. The one on the right gripped up the back of his brother's head and held it there until he was left struggling to breathe and drowning in my juices, which were never in short supply.

Some mighta seen it as a problem. For your nether regions to be a glorified slip and slide. I thought of it as like keeping your car properly oiled so she didn't give out on you. Just like my daddy taught me.

About cars, not my lady bits, you perves.

I leaned my head back, not caring who was doing what anymore as long as they were doing me, tugging on their hair each time one of them tried to pull away. Whoever was currently going down on me ate pussy like a damn felon.

That thought gave me pause. *Were these guys... criminals?*

I lifted my head, and for the first time, I focused on their clothing. Sure, they were dressed a little funny but they didn't look like any criminals I'd ever seen. Then again, Granny always said bad boys ate the best. I was pretty certain she meant food at the time, but it could have been vagina too.

Who was I to judge her senile ass?

"Mmm, fuck!" I squealed with joy, urging the other twin to join his brother.

They were both on me at the same time now, two fingers shoved deep while two tongues flicked my sweet spot.

"Holy fuck! I'm gonna—"

Que's leftover come dribbled out of my mouth and streamed over my chin while my own come splashed onto the faces of the men below me. I scooted back on the chair to get a better look at them. Their smiles were downright devilish, like two boys who knew the only thing they were getting in their stockings on Christmas morning were giant lumps of coal and they couldn't be fucked about it.

They wiped at their mouths and pushed to their feet with mirrored movements. "Mmm, Con, looks like Nickie here just became our *ho, ho, ho* for the holidays."

CHAPTER 8
RUDY

"I know you hear me, hooker!"

I sighed and finally stopped walking, letting Que run his annoying ass right into my back. I knew he would knock me the fuck over, and right now, all I wanted to feel was the pain I deserved for losing sight of Prat. The guys were too busy thinking of how to get their dicks wet, and that left me to keep everyone alive.

Que huffed and scrambled to straddle me on the ground, flipping my body over, despite me being bigger than him and the crazy redhead put together.

Que had the looks, Don and Con had the intensity, Dash and Vix were good with their hands, Blitz was good at... blitzing, Prat knew how to navigate, and I...

I knew how to fuck up.

Maybe I was feeling so on edge because the memories of Holly were pinging around in my head since Que said her name. Maybe it was from being jumped by some horny gremlin the second we sought safety.

Or maybe you're just an idiot, Rudolph.

"C'mon, man. I'm sorry, okay? I know I put my foot in my mouth back there, but I didn't have anything else to work with on short notice."

"You put *your dick* in *her mouth*," I said aloud, watching him trace the tattoos he knew were beneath my shirt with a fingertip.

"Yeah. She's pretty good. Not as good as me, but you should really enjoy the moment and get that delicious cock wet while we wait for Prat to do his thing."

I huffed in a breath, and Que poked at my nipple. Giving me those big, dumb puppy-dog eyes of his.

"Pretty please with a cherry on my cock?"

"I hate you," I mumbled, and he ran his tongue up my neck.

"Oh, I know but your dick sure doesn't, does it, Rue-Rue?"

Despite my irritation, I could feel myself hardening beneath him, my cock ready to give his ass a proper punishment for pissing me off.

"Get off me. We have shit to do."

Que groaned in protest, grinding his thickening cock against mine while rocking his ass back and forth. "*Or...* we could fuck on her decrepit-looking floor and let the rest of the guys keep her occupied?"

I rolled my eyes. "No."

Que grumbled and rolled off me. "Fine. But don't go poking me in the middle of the night when you want your dick in my ass."

I laughed, knowing damn well he wouldn't withhold shit from me and he knew it too. But just to prove a point, I stood up and slammed him into the wall beside a picture frame of the horny redhead and her old-ass grandma.

Watching the shock in Que's eyes as I dragged my lips against his pissed-off ramblings and ground my knee over his cock.

"Keep telling yourself that, Thumper," I hissed into his skin, hearing him moan. "You may just begin to believe it."

His silence had my own cock throbbing in protest when I pulled away from him and his filthy fucking mouth.

"Now. You can pout in a corner and jerk yourself or you can be a good boy and help me map this place out."

"Yeah, yeah, whatever. Clearly you're not going to settle down until we snoop on the poor girl's life."

I nodded, already studying the picture on the wall beside his head. It looked off, but I couldn't tell what was wrong with it through the aged glass. Maybe they got hosed by a bad photo editing job. It's like when you wanted a beach setting but only had a cheap backdrop in your yard to work with.

"Aw. She's sitting with her Granny. Well, looks like that checks out, Grumpy-Pants. What's next?" Que crooned, and I huffed. I didn't trust her. I didn't trust anyone.

"Whatever. There's something off about her."

Que snickered and pinched my ass. "There's something off about you and that's what has me fucking addicted, so stop your complaining. Normal people are boring as fuck. 'Least this one can suck dick."

"Do you ever think with the head on your damn shoulders, asshole?"

I ignored Que's smart-ass remark—I didn't have to hear it to know that's what it would be—and instead went farther down the hallway. My head felt floaty all of a sudden, and I shook it from side to side, trying to clear the fog. All the pent-up anger and frustration must have been starting to get to me.

Happy fucking holidays.

I sighed. Maybe Que was right. Maybe I needed to see this for what it was. This girl, this cabin, could be a change of luck. A gift.

But just like any gift, I wanted to rip it open and see what was hidden inside first.

CHAPTER 9
QUE

Icould hear the twins having fun with Red as I continued to follow Rudy down the hall, picking up the occasional old lady knickknack and picture frame.

Why did old people always have such awful taste in décor? Was it a requirement or something? A starter pack that came with your AARP card?

I flicked a porcelain statue with a tutu while Rudy yanked open a drawer. Guy was convinced something was up with this girl. I was convinced he was just doing what he always did, creating problems where there were none.

It was exactly the reason we spent the last five years behind those bars. Instead of escaping the first chance we got.

I glanced down at the janitor uniform we managed to clip from the old supply closet we found in the basement *more than a year ago* and then up at the back of Rudy's head, enjoying the view of his ass muscles clenching beneath the tight material.

I cocked an eyebrow. *Fucker was a hard ass in more ways than one.*

The last picture frame on a little table outside what appeared to be a bedroom door—a locked bedroom door, if the way Rue-Rue was tugging on it was anything to go by —was one of those old-timey wedding portraits that looked more doom and gloom than my mugshot. And probably a lot like what the fucker in front of me woulda looked like in his own wedding photos.

Rudy wasn't the smiling type.

Okay, that was a lie. He did smile. Once. Shortly after Holly said yes to marrying his dumb ass. I even took a photo as proof. Miracles didn't happen every day. Truth was, there wasn't much I wouldn't do to see him smile like that again...

"Yes?" Rudy repeated, like he wasn't sure he'd heard her right.

"Yes!" Holly nodded, her hands still covering her face the way chicks did when they didn't want you to see their makeup running.

I didn't know what my best friend saw in the woman. She was shallow, and not in the endearing way—like yours truly. In the way that told everyone (but the idiot kneeling at her feet apparently) that she was marrying him for his paygrade.

Rudy wouldn't listen, though. Fucker was "in love."

I downed the rest of the whiskey in my glass, pulled my phone from a pocket, and snapped a quick photo. Not my fault it happened to be at an unflattering angle that gave Holly a double chin. I was just being a good friend and capturing the memory for 'em.

That had been the last time I saw the bitch. Alive anyway. Though I would be the first to admit seeing her dead eyes stare up at me from that hole we dropped her in was about as cathartic as it got.

I set what I was assuming was Grandma's wedding photo back on the table and glanced over to Rudy, who was leaning against the closest wall with his face in his palms.

"Fuck!" Maybe I wasn't the only one reliving ancient history, probably a little more fondly than I should. I rushed over to Rudy, pried his hands back, and realized he had tears in his eyes.

But he wasn't crying. He was laughing. So hard that he *was* crying.

This shit must have really been getting to him. Fucker was losing his damn mind, and I had no clue as to what I could do about it.

Angry Rudy was easy. That anger could be fucked right out of him. But Manic Rudy was a-whole-nother level I'd never stumbled across before.

I gently clamped a hand down on his shoulder, while he threw his thick skull back against the wall with a thud and a laugh. "You okay, man?"

He shook his head. "It's so fucking funny..." he choked out between fits of giggles. The broodiest fucker I'd ever met was... giggling. I think we mighta just stumbled ourselves into an episode of *The Twilight Zone*.

"What is?" I asked, and he pointed to something hanging on the wall across from us. I dropped my hand from his shoulder and stepped closer to get a better look, reading the saying on the crocheted doily thing that was pegged down with a couple of nails directly into the sheetrock, "I wanted to make you something, but I ran out of yar—"

Rudy barked out another loud laugh as soon as I was done speaking. "It's funny... 'cause... 'cause..." He wheezed. "'Cause she couldn't finish the word..." A cough. "Because she ran out of *yarn*."

"Yeah, I got that." I tipped my head to one side to stare at him while he continued to struggle to breathe. A few more seconds and I found myself feeling lighter and laughing too.

Rudy slid down the wall and plopped onto his ass, his legs spread out in front of him and touching the other side of the hallway. "You get it now?"

I mirrored his posture as I scooted over to face him. "You're right. It is fucking funny." At least it was all of a sudden, and I had no clue why.

The commotion had another softer set of footsteps stopping next to us. I followed the bare feet up a pair of leggings to a mop of red hair and then finally a face.

"Hi, Red!" I threw my arms out to the side and accidentally hit my elbow on the little table. "Ow!" I rubbed it a few times before peering up at Nickie again. "You sure are pretty. For a girl."

I stuck my tongue out at her, and Rudy chuckled into his hand. "You said *for a girl*."

Nickie propped her hands on each one of her hips as she looked from me to Rudy. "Did I forget to mention there was a shit-ton of pot in those cookies?"

Rudy laughed, clutched his stomach, and fell onto his side. Staring at me from where he was curled up on the floor. "She gave us pot cookies, Thump—"

"I know," I giggled.

"I don't do drugs," Rudy giggled back.

"Maybe you should start."

CHAPTER 10
NICKIE

I crept across the cold hardwood floor. Pausing when a loose board creaked. "Shhh," I mumbled to myself, mocking Granny's voice. "You're gonna wake the whole damn house, young lady!"

When my foot brushed across a pokey nail, I cursed under my breath and peered over a shoulder. Thing One and Thing Two were passed out on the sofa—one of them had a thumb in his mouth and the other was curled up on his side. Three of the boys were laid out on the living room floor by the fireplace with an empty bottle of liquor we'd found in Granny's cabinet, while the guy who seemed to enjoy weed about as much as I did had fallen asleep in his chair with a joint still in his mouth. It had burned out hours ago but that didn't stop him from sucking on it like a pacifier.

A couple more creaky steps and I found Que and Rudy sleeping on the pull-out sofa Granny kept for guests in her knitting room. I shuffled up to the end of the mattress and stared down at 'em for a few moments.

They sure were pretty. And apparently they thought I was pretty too.

I glanced at myself in the little mirror on the wall while twirling a finger around one of my curls; at the same time my free hand traveled over the rise and fall of my chest and the lines and grooves of my flat stomach under the oversized t-shirt I'd found in Granny's closet and was currently wearing like a nightie. We weren't exactly the same underwear size so I'd go without those, at least until the storm had passed and I could hitch a ride into town. Or maybe one of the boys wouldn't mind takin' me as soon as they got their car patched up.

Que rolled onto his side, drawing my attention from the mirror and back to the bed. He was right. I was pretty. Girl or no girl. And now that he was relaxed a bit, *Big Ol' Broody Rudy* would realize just how much prettier I could be when I was naked.

I tossed Granny's t-shirt off over my head, lifted up the bottom part of the blanket, and crawled up between Rudy's legs. I fit without him even having to move, thanks to the way he'd manspreaded himself across the sheets. Then I slowly picked at the snaps of his onesie until the waistband loosened, reached my hand inside his tighty-whities, and yanked his Coke can of a cock free. A few strokes of my palm and that can was now a two-liter.

Rudy groaned and squirmed, and I dropped my head flat on the mattress and waited for him to stop moving before pushing up on my elbows and giving his tip a long lick. My tongue wiggling it's way against that little come-hole at the end.

"Fuck," he grunted in his sleep, while I tried my darnedest to swallow him down. Your girl might not have much of a gag reflex, but I sure as shit didn't have a soda-bottle-sized vending machine in my throat.

I peered up over Rudy's tree-trunk thigh and watched his hand grasping at the bedsheets, the veins on top dancing and flexing each time he dug his nails farther into the fabric. I grinned around his cock and chugged another inch. Then two. Three. Four. And finally five. The halfway mark.

His ab muscles clenched when he thrusted up into my mouth, and I nearly splattered a night's worth of baked goods back on to his lap. I pulled my head away with a wet plop and caught my breath.

Rudy grumbled something in a sleepy voice, and I strangled his cock by the base to give it a stern talking to. "You and me, we're gonna be good friends, mister, if ya learn how to behave," I whispered before kissing the tip. "See how nice I can be if ya just let me? Now, mind your manners."

I leaned forward again, dropping my jaw as far as it would go, holding my breath, and diving back in.

"Mmm..." Rudy met me with another groan and a thrust. "Thumper..."

"Hm?" Que mumbled back, not bothering to roll over.

I sucked a little harder, and Rudy moaned a whole lot louder. "Just like that."

"Oh yeah, baby—wait, just like what?" Que asked from beside us.

"Keep doing that thing with your tongue."

"What thing?" Que huffed, turning around and pushing upright on the bed. I couldn't see him from where I was still buried under the blanket but I could feel the mattress shifting. "You mean breathing?"

Rudy stiffened beneath me. Well, at least the rest of him stiffened. The bit of him in my mouth was plenty stiff to begin with. Then he was shooting up on the sofa bed and throwing the blanket onto the floor.

He stared down at me while I peered back up at him from where I was kneeling between his thighs. "What the fuck!"

I twirled my tongue around the tip one last time before working it out of my mouth, a spiderweb of spit keeping us connected. "Hi!"

I grinned up at him and then jumped onto his chest much like I'd done outside. Clearly not expecting it, he landed on his back on the mattress with my ass straddling his torso.

"Nickie, what the fuck are you doing?" Rudy grunted from beneath me, doing his best not to touch me but I could see the way his eyes were hinged on my chest.

Oh, so he's a booby dude!

I shrugged a shoulder while reaching up to tweak my own nipples, my pussy leaving a snail mark across his chest as I rotated my hips. "Helping you relax."

"Doesn't get more relaxed than sleeping," Rudy countered, his neck craning slightly to the side so that he could glare at Que while still keeping an eye on me. "A little help?"

Que shook his head, a small smirk telling me I was gonna like his answer much better. "Nope, I think you got this one, baby."

CHAPTER 11
RUDY

Somehow, when I'd envisioned escaping prison with the closest thing I had to a family, I hadn't imagined a persistent redhead waking me from a deep fucking sleep with a blowjob...

The pot was still heavily in my system, and despite my irritation at the little shit, I couldn't help myself. I burst out laughing so hard that the girl on top of me jiggled around like she was riding a bull.

To be fair, I was six-seven with about three-hundred pounds of pure, hard muscle—I had to be with all the shit that was thrown at me. I threw back at it by breaking my body at the gym. After Holly, I didn't feel the need to be some sculpted sex doll like Que. I wanted mass, bulk, and a "bubbly" personality to persuade everyone to leave me the fuck alone.

Apparently *this girl* didn't understand *that*.

"Get. Off," I grunted.

"I'm trying, silly!" She giggled and rubbed her hips over my dick, and I groaned.

"C'mon, Rue-Rue. She's like a Christmas tree!" Que chimed in from the peanut gallery.

"You mean the pathetic shrub in her living room...?" I ground out.

"Yeah, she sparkles on the outside. She's kinda dead on the inside, and she looks good with balls on her!" Que snickered, and I bit my lip when she rubbed against me harder.

Fuck, it had been so fucking long since a chick bounced on my cock. And this bitch could handle a third of it. Just a little less than Que himself.

"Hey, I have an idea, boys," Nickie said, her green eyes flickering in a way that admittedly got me harder.

"Oh yeah? What's that, Red?" Of course Que heard *game* and perked up like a salivating mutt, his tongue out and his dick wagging.

"A sexy game. For the holidays, ya know? Gran always said the best way to spread holiday cheer was by—"

"—spreading your legs and assaulting sleeping men?" I finished for her, but Nickie laughed like it was what she meant to say all along.

"C'mon, sourpuss," Que whined, already pulling his dick out of his underwear and reaching for my hand.

I hesitated when he put my palm on Nickie's bare chest. Her breasts were amazing if I were being honest with myself—better than Holly's deflated balloons, that was for sure. "Listen, I think we should—"

"Okay! Truth or dare, Que?" Nickie squealed and clapped her hands together.

Que stroked himself absently and watched me as he answered, "Dare."

Nickie giggled, looking mischievous while doing some

weird dance on my lap. "*You* kiss *him*!" She gestured a finger between us.

The girl didn't know our... relations. So she must have thought she was being fucking sneaky. Que and I were thinking the same thing, because he cocked a grin that said it all before gripping my throat and bringing my lips against his in a dominating kiss.

Normally I fought the fucker for control. But tonight, with this flighty feeling in my veins, I enjoyed letting him lead. Nickie rocked against me, her clit brushing the base of my cock in a way that had her whimpering.

Que didn't give me a minute to breathe, devouring the fuck out of my mouth and moaning when he bit my bottom lip. "Give me a challenge, why don't you?"

"Broody Rudy!" Nickie panted, her wetness seeping into my skin. I could smell it. "Your turn. Truth or dare?"

I sighed and reluctantly agreed to play her childish games. "Truth."

"Boooo!" Que whined and laughed to himself.

"Hmm, okay. Who's your favorite person in the whole wide world?" Nickie stretched her arms out to the sides, like I needed the visual.

The name came to my lips without thought, the weed acting as some sort of stupid truth serum. "Quentin. Most days anyway."

Nickie caught the slip and her green eyes narrowed slightly. "Not your fiancée?"

I went silent but Que didn't miss a beat. "Bros before hoes, babe. Now, that's enough with the games."

Nickie squeaked when Que gripped her hair and yanked her forward into a kiss that rivaled the one he gave me. I tried to get up, but I was ignored. He grabbed for

Nickie's hand and placed it on that fucking spot right under my balls.

"Oh, fuck—"

"Mmm. That's right, Rue-Rue." Que smiled triumphantly. "Now c'mon, Red, rock back and forth on his thick cock. He'll be a good boy for you. I promise."

Nickie and I moaned in unison as she followed Que's instructions to the fucking T. I couldn't help myself. Between the way the fucker was looking at me as he stroked his cock and she rocked against me, I was a goner.

"Fine. You want it, little shit? Let's see if you can take it." I didn't give her a minute to breathe or to adjust. I picked her tiny ass off my stomach and slammed her down onto my cock.

Que groaned louder, watching me fuck this girl like I'd done to him so many times before.

"Don't go easy on her, baby. Make her work for it," Que moaned as he positioned himself behind Nickie and pressed her down while I drove up into her surprisingly-tight cunt.

"Ah! Fucking hell, you're a mammoth, Soda Pop! I'm so full!" she screamed, and I snorted. That wasn't exactly the best compliment I'd gotten about my size, but at least it was original.

"Yeah he is, Red," Que agreed, swatting her left cheek. "Lift this nice little ass for me. So we can show you what full really feels like."

CHAPTER 12
NICKIE

"**H**oly fucking fuck, fuck, fuuuuuck!"

Que shoved his cock into my ass while Soda Pop continued to plow my pussy. I couldn't breathe, much less move. I'd lost count of how many times they'd made me come already. I was a one-thruster buster. But c'mon! Who the hell wouldn't be when you had two large servings of sausage stuffed into your holes.

I could see Gran's face, all disapproving and grumpy, kinda like Rudy when he wasn't balls-deep inside my pussy.

Rudy made a growly noise low in his throat, and Que locked his large hands around my mouth from behind before dropping his lips to my ear. "Such a good fucking girl for us. Don't scream or you'll get more than your little stocking can handle."

I whimpered at the thought of *all of them...* I wasn't ready for that. But damn, did my vagina weep for it.

"Shhh!" I grumbled through his hands. "Or you'll be the ones waking them."

The boys quieted and continued pounding me. Que was the first to come. His thick spurts leaking down my asshole and coating Grumpy's balls—though he didn't seem to mind too much. In fact, Soda Pop fucked me harder, flipping me around so he could do me doggy style while leaning forward to suck our combined juices from the source.

Watching a dude suck off another dude, especially these delicious morsels of man meat, was enough to make me orgasm again.

"Oh fuck! Yes! Yes! Yes! Suck him clean. Open wider. Suck—"

Rudy plowed me so hard white spots danced like ornaments in front of my eyes, and I couldn't help but scream. Even though I knew I was supposed to be quiet.

"You don't get to tell me what to do. Shut that pretty mouth or I'll make you choke on his fucking cock," he hissed.

Someone was being a bit of a grinch, but like every toxic man, I could fix him.

I opened my mouth wider and looked them both in the eye, letting my brat flag fly high.

Que chuckled, moving to where he could link his fingers in my hair, and yanked my face down to slob on his juicy knob. Rudy licked most of the come off him already, but I could still taste it, along with all the saliva.

"So greedy, aren't you, Red?" Que said, and I moaned in response, vibrating the head of his cock while reaching around to knead his balls.

Rudy was grunting behind me, thrusting harder and faster till I swore I might break in two. *Ow. But a good ow?*

"Where do you want his come? Where do you think you deserve it?" Que asked. "Choose wisely."

"I am not coming inside her," Rudy protested, as he got closer and closer to that edge. I could feel him shaking.

Mmm, we'll see about that. Babies were cute. Maybe a broody baby from Rudy wouldn't be such a bad idea after all. I could name it after my sister. Or Granny. Or...

Rudy started to pull away, but I locked his ass down with my legs, pushing him into the mattress harder so that his dick was locked inside me like a bone stuck in a garbage disposal.

"Agh! Nickie, don't—"

Que's jaw dropped in shock, and I just smiled, sticking my finger into his mouth and swirling it around.

"What the fuck!" Rudy barked, all but throwing me off when he was done exploding the top off his dick, his not so teeny-weeny sperm bubbles dripping their way down my thighs.

CHAPTER 13
QUE

Rudy shot me one of his notorious *melt a hole through your forehead* glares before stomping out of the old lady's knitting room with a sheet wrapped around his waist—his jumpsuit had made it to the floor along with his underwear at some point. I heard the bathroom door slam and then the running of water.

Normally I'd join him. But lukewarm showers weren't my thing any more than being the target of his moods were *after* he'd already busted a nut.

I looked over to Nickie who was twirling around the room again, Rudy's come dripping down her legs like a victory flag.

Victory puddle? Was that a thing? She sure as shit made it look like a thing.

The big guy was right. There was something wrong with that girl but not in the way he was suggesting. She wasn't dangerous—I didn't think. Just off her rocker, in the *she had a few of the screws in her head fucked loose* way. And I didn't mind knocking around a few more.

We had time to kill, seeing as that storm wasn't letting up. I just hoped Prat appeared soon, or Rudy was going out there, blizzard or not.

Nickie started humming to herself, and my eyes bounced from her tits to my cock, which was already at half-mast again. I coaxed her forward with a twitch of my finger, and she got on her knees and crawled towards me. Stopping when she was positioned between my thighs.

Rudy didn't call me Thumper for no reason. I fucked like a rabbit, and deep down, he loved that about me. Our new friend here didn't seem to mind it either.

I wrapped a hand around a fistful of red hair and yanked her head back so that I was staring into a pair of emerald-green eyes. Eyes that twinkled like a string of Christmas lights as she smiled up at me while I slowly lowered her face closer to my cock.

She'd just closed her dick-swollen lips around the top when the hallway light flickered. A second later, the entire cabin went dark. Then a loud banging sound, followed by a barrage of Rudy-laden curses came from the direction of the bathroom.

Nickie jumped up off the floor and ran towards the chaos, bare-assed and unbothered, as I tugged on a pair of underwear I thought were mine and rushed after her.

"Hold up, Red Racer!"

By the time I caught up to her, she was standing in the bathroom while Rudy laid cock-up in the bottom of her Granny's clawfoot tub. I could just make out the shape of him with the moonlight reflecting off the snow piled high next to the tiny window. One foot tangled in a broken shower curtain and the other suspended in the air like one of those old *I've fallen and can't get up* commercials.

I extended an arm, and he grabbed on to my elbow while I helped tug him to his feet. "Think we lost power." I grinned.

"You don't say," he grunted back.

"Hey, Soda Pop, you don't have a fiancée, do ya?" Nickie asked as Rudy shoved past *me* to get as far away from *her* as the confined space would let him.

"Not anymore, I don't..." he grumbled.

I slung an arm around her shoulder and lowered my mouth to her ear. "Pretty sure you made the big guy's naughty list this year, babe."

"I never was good at, well, being good." She shrugged.

I guided Nickie out to the living room, where Rudy seemed to be doing a head count. Nine warm bodies, with a crazy ginger in our ranks instead of Prat.

"We need candles, flashlights, batteries, an inventory of what food we have on hand—perishable versus nonperishable—and more kindling for the fireplace as soon as first light hits."

This was where our fearless leader thrived. Throw a natural disaster at the guy and he was on top of his game. Lock him in a room with someone of the female persuasion and not so much.

"Nickie," Rudy barked. Neither one of us had been paying attention as her fingers were dipping into my underwear while the hand I had draped around her shoulders was twisting one of her nipples. "Candles, flashlights, batteries—*now*."

"Sir, yes, sir." She jumped to attention, chest out and all, before pivoting on a heel and disappearing down a set of stairs off the kitchen. I could hear skipping down the steps. I could also hear her trip and crash into a pile of boxes.

"Go with her." Rudy cocked his head in my direction.

"Creepy-ass basements are more of a Blitz thing." I pointed across the room. Blitz's shadow looked to me and shook its head. "Twins?" I tried again and got a...

"No." And a... "Fuck no."

Dane and Dash were tucking themselves behind furniture like I couldn't see two giant blobs larger than the width of the sofa, and that's when my sights settled on Vix, who was either too blind or dumb to realize what was going on right now.

I dropped down next to him on the sofa, grabbed his arm and shoved until he was up on his feet. "The hot chick needs your help in the basement."

"What hot chick?" he mumbled, scratching his balls before stretching his arms over his head. I could still smell the liquor on his breath. Moonshine, if I were to hazard a guess. No wonder the fucker didn't know his ass from a hole in the ground.

"The redhead with the big tits." I pointed to the basement door. "She's all alone down there without a cock to keep her company. You're up, brother." I gave his ass a few quick taps, and Vix stumbled towards the door.

"He's more likely to take a long trip down a short flight of stairs than she is," Rudy grumbled at me.

I lifted a shoulder. "More food for the rest of us then."

"Which reminds me..." Rudy clapped his hands together, suddenly forgetting he was standing in the middle of the room with that same bedsheet still wrapped around his waist. "Everyone up and start taking a stock count."

CHAPTER 14
NICKIE

Five. Four. Three. Two. One...

I counted off in my head, waiting for the shadowy figure to cautiously make its way down the stairs, and when he finally reached the landing, I jumped out and screamed "boo" as loud as I could.

The figure dropped ass-first onto the bottom step with a bang and a grunt. I laughed, pulled the old clown mask I found in one of Granny's boxes of junk up off my head, and tossed it aside. She had a tub labeled for every holiday. Including more Christmas stuff I could bring upstairs.

"Got ya!" I aimed a finger at him.

"Ow, fuck," he grunted back, and I dusted away a couple of cobwebs and flicked on the little flashlight I swiped off the back shelf and shined it in his direction. Taking in the sharp lines of his jaw, dark shaggy hair, and bright blue eyes, which he was having trouble keeping open with the way I was blinding him.

"My bad." I lowered the handle of the flashlight and helped Drunky to his feet. I might not have remembered his name, but I sure as shit remembered how much he liked Granny's moonshine. "Which one are you again?" I asked him.

He opened his mouth to answer and ended up stumbling forward. The blow sent us both tumbling back into another stack of boxes before he rolled us over so that he was spread out on the cold cement floor underneath my naked ass.

"Vix," he said while staring up at me with a dopey grin. All lips and teeth. But nice lips and teeth. Plump pussy-sucking lips and white booby-biting teeth.

I trailed a finger over the outline of his pecs and lower to his ab muscles. I could feel his heart beating in his chest. "Well, Vix, how about you and me get to know each other a little better?"

He swallowed and nodded as I reached into the tub of Christmas decorations I'd pulled out from under the stairs and tugged a string of red-and-green tree lights free. Stretching Vix's hands high above his head and wrapping his wrists up prettier than a present. It was like having my own life-sized GI Joe. All that was missing was the bow.

Aw, Granny, you shouldn't have! Then again, I was a very, very good girl this year. Despite what I told Que. Just depended on your definition of "good." Mine leaned a little more towards the good at being bad side of things.

I reached behind me, slipped a hand into Vix's pants, and fished around until I felt what I was looking for. Or more like didn't feel.

I scrunched up my nose, clamping a hand over his mouth when he went to offer me what I could only assume was an excuse. "Shhh, it's okay. We ain't gonna let a little thing like whiskey dick stop us from having fun, now are we?"

I shook my head, squeezing his cheeks and forcing him to shake his along with me.

"That's what I thought." I grinned and shimmied higher on his waist, straddling his shoulders and pressing on the meat of his jaw until his mouth was opening and I was lowering myself down on top of it.

The first swipe of his tongue on my clit told me I wasn't taking V's oral V-card, while the splattering of something wet and globby on his chin reminded me he was eating his friend's come.

The thought just made me wetter as I continued to grind my pussy up and down and side to side. My hands digging in his hair and jerking his head whichever way felt better in the moment.

Sometimes I liked it sloppy, uncoordinated, and teasing. Other times I wanted to get straight to the point. Right now was one of those *other* times, so I pulled harder on his hair. Forcing his tongue out and his chin up and started to ride his face. All my leverage gone when my stomach clenched and my upper body arched forward. My palms flat on the floor by each side of his head and my bare knees raw as I continued to scrape away at layer after layer of skin.

I wouldn't say that I was a sex addict. It wasn't sex that I enjoyed. It was the orgasms. The power that came with them. Whether it was me or someone else achieving them. The way that every part of me or them was controlled by what was being done to it. Watching the eyes roll back, a cock stiffen, feeling your pussy salivate, your body convulse. It was nature's drug. And it was free.

At least for me it was. I was sure some people paid for it. But my ass never had to.

Vix groaned against my pussy lips, the vibration traveling up inside me and curling the tips of my toes. And I could feel it. That perfect balance of coming and not coming. The point of no return. It was like a needle to my vein. A flash and a bang. Hot and cold. Building up and letting go.

"Will you two dumbasses stop fucking around and get your asses up here," Rudy called down the stairs.

"We're coming!" I called back with a giggle.

Well, I was coming. My new friend here still couldn't get it up.

I grabbed on to his limp biscuit anyway, stroking it through the fabric of his pants, and a few more back-and-forth motions and twists of my hips had a familiar warmth flooding my belly and pouring over into Vix's mouth. He swallowed it all down like a good boy. He had to or he'd drown.

I gave his cheek a little pat as a reward before jumping to my feet and leaving him tied up on the floor, remembering to snatch the flashlight and the extra box of Christmas decorations.

Granny didn't decorate so much anymore. But that was before we had a whole house full of guests to entertain.

CHAPTER 15
RUDY

The crazy bitch that is Nickie Unknown-Last-Name ran past me in a blur with a big-ass box in her hands as I made my way down the steps.

I knew these morons weren't going to get anything done. *Why was I the only one with any brain cells left?*

Vix was on the ground, struggling with what looked to be a tangle of Christmas lights. He'd gotten his foot caught near his hands while trying to push them off.

I leaned against the wall, watching him grunt and struggle with his dick half flopped out of his pants and softer than a noodle.

"Better watch out, Vix. Getting tangled up with our little Saint Nickie is a bad idea."

Vix looked up at me and grunted, clearly unable to free himself from the contorted pose I wasn't certain he could do if he were sober.

"Can you yell at me *after* getting these damn things off me, oh mighty overlord?"

I snorted but leaned down to work the lights off his

body. When he got to his feet, he grumbled and skulked back up the stairs without so much as a *thank you*.

This chick would be the death of us...

Of course, Nickie and Vix didn't bother grabbing anything I actually fucking asked for so I was now going to have to do it myself. And seeing as this wasn't my cabin, I didn't even know where to start, much less in the damn dark with piles of junk stacked up in every corner. I could hear Nickie giggling with the morons upstairs as I tried navigating the small space with only the help of the moon-light streaming in from the single window.

"Ow! Fucking perfect," I said, bashing my head against a shelf too low for my stature. I was used to smacking into ceiling fans and doorframes—it came with being tall—but not at full speed, for lack of a better word. "Nickie!" I hollered, holding my throbbing temple and tucking my dick aside to keep it away from the rabid sex demon.

I really needed to find my briefs...

Didn't her cunt hurt yet? I felt my dick tear her open. Maybe the chick was a masochist. No wonder the boys loved her.

A few minutes later, Nickie hopped down the stairs like a damn child, the wall illuminated by the flashlight in her hand.

"Why didn't you grab anything I asked for?"

The little shit shined the light in my face, blinding me. "I did! See?"

I rolled my eyes before flicking towards the aftermath of Christmas lights Vix had left on the floor.

"Jealous I didn't tie you up too?" Nickie's green eyes shined with mischief, and I swear I could see some hidden gleam of evil in their depths.

"Fuck no. Try that shit on me and I'll wrap it around your throat."

Nickie giggled and twirled around before shining the damn flashlight right in my face again. "Oh, kinky, I like it!"

I quirked a brow, then shook my head, bringing a hand to my forehead to block the beam. "Stop blinding me, or I'll take it away."

Nickie pouted, adjusting the light and giving me a mock salute. "Yes, Daddy."

"For fuck's sake. Just tell me where we can find rations, additional light, and some form of protection!"

"Why?"

"In case... uh... In case there are wolves out there."

"Wolves?" she repeated, all stupid and doe-eyed. "And how should I know where that stuff is? Look in the boxes."

This woman was trying my patience by breathing. "It's your house. How do you *not* know?"

"Nope! It's *Gran's* house."

I was literally face-palming at this point. "And she didn't tell you where she keeps her shit before you got here?"

Nickie chewed on her lip and looked around nervously. It lasted a split second before she perked up and started dancing again, making herself dizzy from the light bouncing all around. "No, silly. Granny... doesn't talk much anymore."

Hmm, was the old lady sick? Maybe Nickie stole this property from right under her grandmother's nose.

I rummaged through boxes, trying to put my hands on anything but Nickie's damn neck. I found a shit-ton of yarn and thought of Que, pocketing a handful to throw at him later.

"You look hot when you're all broody."

I could feel her shadow on my back as I stood to my full height, quickly remembered to duck down, and turned around. Resting a palm on Nickie's forehead before she got any closer to me. "Fuck no. You got plenty of toys upstairs who are more than willing to play your twisted game. I've got work to do."

She huffed, her lower lip quivering until I gave her head a light shove.

"Now, little shit. Go upstairs and keep the boys warm. I'll be back when I've dug out enough supplies. And leave this—" I snatched the flashlight from her hand and spun her body towards the stairs, finishing her off with a little kick to her ass.

I shook my head as I watched her skip away.

Good luck, boys. She's your fucking problem now.

CHAPTER 16
NICKIE

"Eeny, meeny, miney..." I said, prancing upstairs and observing the boys.

The twins were cuddled together in a blanket, laughing over old comics with boobies on them. They got mad at me earlier and told me they weren't called *that*. They were manga. If I was going to be ridiculed my whole life for liking romance books, I was going to call it like I sees it: *book porn*.

Nothing wrong with it, but don't go lyin'.

Vix was nursing another bottle, and I vaguely wondered how many we even had left in Granny's fridge. He'd already hit the hard stuff.

None of them were paying much mind to me, not even Que, and he always wanted to fuck. I was feeling a little sore but the best way to cure the pain was to become numb to it.

Blitz had a joint he'd rolled pretty fantastically with the shit he must have found in one of Granny's hidey holes.

I could use a good smoke. Maybe he'd be nicer than the grump downstairs.

"Mo!" I cheered excitedly, plopping down on the couch. Jostling Blitz and his blunt and watching ash fall onto his exposed torso. He had his weird onesie thingy pulled down off his arms and tied at his waist, showing me the happiest of trails.

"'Sup? You sure light up the room, don't ya?"

I beamed at him, snagging the joint and taking a massive drag that had the end smoldering with an orange glow. It was a *bit* too much and I gagged, which caused Blitz to laugh his ass off. The others didn't notice, busy with burning random crayons Rudy told them to light in different areas of the cabin.

They better not go in Gran's room. She didn't like people going in there.

"What's the matter?" Blitz said with a laugh. "Can't take it, *little star*? Here, lemme help you out."

He swiped his joint back, and I glared at him. That was... until he gripped my cheeks and brought his lips to mine, blowing a thick cloud of smoke into my mouth. My pussy clenched, and I couldn't keep my hands off him, despite still being irritated by his jab.

"Oh, shit. You got the good stuff," I hummed in approval.

He laughed. "You mean *you* got the good stuff. So high you forgot or something?"

"Or something." I shrugged, dragging his lips to my neck and sliding my fingers down to his dick in his onesie.

"Mmm, naughty girl. If you don't stop, you're gonna make me blow my sack. But that's what you want, isn't it?"

I smiled as I lowered my mouth onto his lap, popping his dick out of his outfit and using the bottom snap to hold him in place for me. But I wasn't interested in just licking his popsicle stick. He was my *mo*, yes, but he was an eeny meeny before that. Now was my chance to return the favor.

"Oh fuck. Nobody touches my balls usually. That feels good."

I could vaguely see the guys staring at us now, watching through the low flickers of the makeshift crayon candles that were surprisingly useful.

Guess Rudy wasn't just good for a rippingly fun fuck after all. Bravo, Soda Pop.

Que had his hands in his pants, not bothering to hide the fact he was peeping on us, and I moaned, my eyes beckoning him closer.

"C'mere. Suck his cock for me, Rabbit Man. I wanna show him something else."

Que quirked a brow at me, but he listened like the good little bunny that he was and hopped on over to the couch, following my direction again when I used my bare foot to lower him to his knees before joining him between his friend's legs.

"Don't come in my mouth, Blitz. You know I get nauseous from the texture," Que warned, and I eyed him for a moment.

He hadn't seemed all that bothered by Rudy's...

"Take this off, Smokey," I said, letting my voice dip low and get all porn star like.

Gran's picture frame was above my head, and I smirked at her while watching Que help ditzy Blitzy get buck naked.

"Such a good boy." I purred when Blitz reclaimed his spot on the couch, spreading his legs wide for me and Que.

I gave him a quick kiss that got his lips nice and slippery and then lowered his head down onto Blitz's dick. At least this one was hard. Giving a quick pointed look to Nancy Drunk in the corner still nursing the neck of the vodka bottle, I slipped my fingers in my mouth.

The twins had their dicks in their hands again, leisurely stroking from tip to base and filling the room with soft pants that made me tingle. Hell, even Dash and Dane were grinding against each other without realizing it as they watched my perfectly orchestrated performance.

Blitz still had the joint in his mouth, sucking on the filter like it was a lifeline, and I knew it was the right time.

Wickedly grinning and rightfully earning my naughty list crown, I slipped a hand under Blitzy's balls and found his pucker. A soft, surprised squeak barely left his lips before I shoved two fingers knuckle-deep into his netherworld and curled them towards myself.

"Oh—fuck!" He squealed higher than I thought a man could squeal, and Que started choking. He popped off at the same time white come began spewing all over Blitz's lap and the couch.

Oh, Granny's gonna be mad now...

"What's the matter?" I grinned, meeting Blitz right in his meenie eyes and watching him hack and sputter. "Can't handle it?"

QUE

ell, that ended a little prematurely.

I wiped the excess saliva from the sides of my mouth with the back of a hand and pushed to my feet, my knees buckling out from under me for a sec. This chick had a sex drive that rivaled my own and my body was starting to feel the consequences.

Yeah, you're not the only one who's shocked. But there was a lot going out and not so much coming in—if ya catch my drift.

My stomach grumbled, reminding me the last full meal we'd all had was a plate of baked beans and some stale bread that we'd washed down with a gallon of powdered drink mix.

Sure, the cookies had been a nice dose of sugar we weren't used to having. But right now, we all needed some real food. And probably some that contained a little less pot. Except for Rue-Rue... Loved the guy but *he needed* to chill, enjoy himself, stop clattering around the basement like we had a bunch of armed guards at our door.

The storm did more than buy us time. It covered our

tracks, and Prat'd already told us this cabin wasn't on the maps. No address meant no GPS location meant no tracking us down.

Besides, we all knew how the politics of this shit worked. It was easier to mark us as DOA than to spend more of the tax payers cash trying to hunt us down. It saved 'em all face too, kept the warden from having to admit a group of convicted felons had gotten out on his watch.

Blitz groaned and cleaned himself up with one of the decorative pillows the old lady of the house had tossed onto the couch, just as Rudy was barreling back up the stairs again with a string of Christmas lights tossed over a shoulder and a couple of boxes in his arms.

He looked from Blitz, to me, and back over to Nickie —who was twirling around the kitchen in nothing but an apron now. I didn't know what she thought she was making in the dark without any electricity, but she was taking bowls out of cabinets and had grabbed the warm milk from the fridge and set it out by the sink next to a box of pancake mix.

Rudy dropped the boxes on the floor with a loud plop, as daylight finally started streaming in from the wall of windows behind me. My guess? It was nearly seven in the morning, and we'd all slept for maybe four hours.

"What she do now?" Rudy grunted, and Blitz just grinned in reply. "Right, that's what I thought."

The big guy continued to mumble something about *not getting shit done with our dicks all out* before stalking over to Nickie, grabbing her by the wrists and tugging her back into the living room. Not all that unwillingly, though. Seeing as the nutter was giggling along the way.

He then proceeded to take the Christmas lights from his shoulder and toss them in the air, waiting for the cable to catch on one of the rafters. He tugged on the shorter end until he'd fashioned himself a pulley system, snatching up Nickie's wrists again, wrapping them in the cord, and yanking until they were high above her head and she was suspended on her tiptoes, while she smiled through it all.

"Careful, Soda Pop. I'm ticklish!" she called out at him as he took the other side of the pulley and attached it to a hook on the wall.

"Won't be so ticklish when I'm done with you." He ground his teeth and kneeled behind her.

"While you're down—"

Her taunt was severed by a squeal when he took a little green bulb from the leftover string of lights and shoved it up her ass, feeding a few more inches into her hole before wrapping the loose ends around her neck and wrists. Then he jumped to his feet and whispered next to her ear. "I wouldn't clench if I were you. The glass is fragile. Now. Stay. The fuck. Still."

He didn't bother waiting for her to answer before storming off towards the kitchen. Not that the girl seemed fazed. He was trying for tough love, but all I think he was doing was turning her on more.

There was just something about redheads that came with a side of daddy issues and a pain kink. Our nymphy little hostess was all that and more.

Rudy glanced around at the stash of cans the twins had piled up on the counter, appearing to do the math in his head. "We got about a day's worth of dry goods between us. Maybe two," he said more to himself as he paused to draw a rusty-looking hatchet from his back. "Looks like we're going hunting, boys." He waved the sharp end from Dash to Dane. "You two can stay behind and keep an eye on *her*."

Vix whined, and Rudy stifled it with a glare.

"A little bit of cold will help your ass sober the fuck up."

The rest of us started putting on our socks and shoes—we'd left them drying by the fireplace overnight—and snatching up various weapons and old tools Rudy had scavenged up in the basement.

Just as I was about to make my way towards the door with a chopping axe in tow, Rudy tugged me back by the collar. "I don't trust her," he grunted into my ear.

We each peered over into the living room, watching Red bounce on her toes while singing some Christmas song to herself. I recognized the tune but not the words. I was pretty sure she was making those up on her own.

"So you've mentioned." I turned, clamped a hand down on Rudy's shoulder, and gave it a slight squeeze. "You're starting to sound like a broken record, man."

He shrugged, forcing me to drop my hand. "And you're starting to sound like an asshole."

He stormed past me and I called out after him, "Just starting?"

CHAPTER 18
NICKIE

"O n the second day of Christmas, Granny gave to me..." I hummed to myself. "...an Eiffel Tower and a couple of beefcakes doing the deed..."

One of the beefcakes in question—the one with the scar over his eyebrow and hair shaved down to his head—looked to his counterpart before smiling at me.

"You need some attention, sweetheart?" he asked, cocking his head to the side. He didn't wait for me to answer before he was kicking his feet off the coffee table and approaching me like the coyote tryin' to catch the roadrunner. Predator to prey. 'Cept I'd never been very good at being the prey.

I nodded as he reached out a hand and flicked one of my hardened nipples through the fabric of Granny's apron. She claimed they were flowers. They looked more like vaginas to me.

She wouldn't appreciate me wearing it right now. Her favorite apron. Especially with what I hoped was coming. Me, again. Them too, probably. Maybe. But I didn't really care what the old grinch thought about me anymore. I was having too much fun while her vagina had shriveled up and dusted over a while ago. She really did just need to loosen up, stop being so stiff.

It was my firm belief that every bat was just one good orgasm away from feeling young at heart. And I had plenty of 'em to go around.

I wonder if any of the boys had a thing for older women? Sharing was caring after all.

As if reading my mind, Scar Face glanced towards his friend again and smirked. Couldn't see his lips, but I could see the way his Adam's apple twitched in his throat. "Hey, Dash, come give me a hand."

Or cock. Or mouth. I wasn't picky.

The second guy shook his head from side to side. "Rudy said not to fuck with her, man."

"No, he said to keep our eyes on 'er." Scar Face turned back in my direction, a delicious smirk tipping up one side of his mouth. He was definitely into older women. I could just tell. "He didn't mention keeping anything else *off* her."

"Pretty please." I stuck out my bottom lip while fluttering my eyelashes as I spun around on my toes. I was starting to make myself dizzy. "It sure is lonely *hanging* around all by my lonesome."

"Ya hear that, man?" Scar Face called out again. "She's lonely. A girl as pretty as she is should never feel lonely. It's ungentlemanlike. Didn't your ma raise ya to be a gentleman?"

"Uh, yeah, she sure did." Dash nodded, taking a few tentative steps in my direction while his friend nudged a kitchen chair across the room, scooting it over until it was close enough for me to climb on one knee at a time. My bare ass popped in the air and my chest propped up over the top rail. "But if this goes south, you're dealing with Rudy, Dane."

"If this goes south, *Que* is dealing with Rudy," Scar Face shot back.

I heard his pants hit the floor and then he was pressing up behind me, his cock tapping on my ass and splattering a hefty dab of precum on each cheek. I could feel the Christmas lights peeking out and slithering back in each time I took a deep breath. Like a morbid game of Pop goes the Weasel. In this case, *I* was the weasel, and we didn't want anything popping.

The thought should have been intimidating. It wasn't. It was hot. The added bit of danger making my pussy leak down my thighs.

Dane slowly edged his way inside me, careful not to dislodge the bulbs whenever he slid back out again. And I moaned as Dash pulled his cock out of his pants and leveled it with my face. I was too high up to do much more than lick the tip a few times. But that seemed to be enough to have the guy in front of me groaning and stroking himself in rhythm with his friend's awkward thrusts.

In and out and back and forth. Lick, thrust. Thrust, lick. I continued to rock forward like a pendulum, the chair legs creaking beneath me and the string of Christmas lights groaning above me as the plastic chafed against the rafters.

Dane started rocking me harder, no longer seeming all that concerned about the bulb the closer he got to nutting. I felt the first crack and something sharp around the outside of my asshole, a jagged edge at the same time I heard a snap. And then my arms were slumping against my shoulders. One end of the cord cracking back and popping Dane in the face while my chair toppled forward into Dash.

I tumbled over him, rolled onto my side, and untwisted the cable from around my wrist before carefully removing the cracked bulb from my ass. It was just a small nick, barely any blood as I grabbed a pair of boots I found next to the fireplace, ducked and made a mad dash for the door, just as a *mad* Dash lunged for me.

I shoved my feet into the too-big-for-me boots and rushed out into the snow. Granny's apron billowing behind me as the first frosty breeze curled my toes. It was so cold I could barely breathe but it was exhilarating at the same time.

"Ut-oh! Too slow!" I giggled as I dove behind a tree, peeking out to watch the boys standing by the door and looking from side to side. I glanced at Dash's shoeless feet and watched him curse under his breath as he dipped one of his socks into the snow. He pulled it back again and stepped closer to the cabin.

It wouldn't be hard to track me with the little trail of blood I was leaving behind but it sure was entertaining to scoop up snowballs into a pile until they did.

CHAPTER 19
RUDY

"This should be sufficient," I said, assessing the piles of meat we'd collected over the last few hours. The others were still trying to find game, but Que and I had a metal pail full of fish and downed two bucks on our own.

It was hard enough to hunt half sleep-deprived and waiting for a damn sniper to end us like the prey we chased. But we also had to fight the fact we didn't have much winter gear at our disposal.

Que finished deboning the head of his buck. We couldn't properly drain them so we were covered in blood. I stared at the lake in front of us. I considered jumping in, for no reason other than to wash off, but I didn't want my nuts shriveled up into a couple of acorns so I continued to slice away at the meat, not having a choice but to leave the skin for lack of proper tools.

"What do you think they're up to?" Que asked, bashing the fish in the head one by one with a sizable rock.

I thought about Nickie, tied up and docile for fucking

once. "Fuck if I know... or care. They better keep their dicks to themselves, though, or I'll cut them the fuck off."

Que hissed between his teeth, closing his legs and wincing at the imagery I was painting for him. "Damn, what's your damage against Red? So she puts the ho in *holidays*. I'm your whore every day of the year and you love me."

I grunted in response, ignoring his batting eyelashes. "Already told you, I don't trust the little shit."

Something was off with her. She was using sex as a distraction and my crew was all too willing to join in.

"Oh, not this again, man. C'mon, Rue-Rue. Give her some slack. She did welcome nine convicts into her home out of the goodness of her heart."

"Eight," I corrected him, rubbing my chest at the mention of Prat. That dickhead better be okay. "And I don't think her *heart* was the part of her that handled the decision-making when she let a bunch of dicks inside."

Que snickered and stroked his cock with the back of his knuckles, trying to avoid the blood. He wasn't as greased up in the shit as I was. But he did stink like fish after a few hours of splitting the labor.

"You're still worried about Prat, aren't you?" Que came up behind me and began working on my shoulders, likely using my jumper as a damn rag since he had a texture thing.

"Yes. It's my fault. No man left behind. I didn't look for him..."

Que grabbed under my chin, forcing me to twist my neck and look at him. "You aren't responsible for the world, Rudolph. You gotta remember that."

I sighed, ignoring the fact he was coddling me right

now and instead leaned into his touch, feeling the warmth of his skin. I closed my eyes to breathe in his scent. It was fucking cold and just as fishy as I thought it would be but that was Que.

"I got you. You got me. Together we got the boys. We can take on anything, okay, killer? No red-headed horn dog will take us down."

I felt his lips press into mine, and I opened my mouth instinctively like so many times before. It felt so natural now. Guess it always did. I'd just not been in the right headspace to admit it. Que was my safe place. The one person I truly needed to protect. He saved me all those years ago, when I was going to turn myself in for Holly's death. He saved me, and it doomed us both.

Fucking hounds. I could still hear them, sniffing and growling like we were nothing but slabs of meat. Mutts needed to be piked like the fish.

Fucking Nickie too.

Que met my aggression, kissing me deeper.

"We have work to do... We can't..." I protested against his ravaging lips, which kept wrenching groans from deep within my throat.

I was lost in the feel of him when all of a sudden he pulled away, and the light shone over my closed eyes with his absence.

"Wha..?" I mumbled, blinking when a large object smashed me over the head.

My eyes were open now but I could barely see out of the slits in front of them. The fucker had stuck a damn deer skull on me like a mask, complete with the fucking antlers and all. It was skinned down to the bone and smelled like snow and blood.

"Are you serious?" I grunted, picking up a fish from the bucket and flipping it around in my hand while Que continued to laugh his ass off. I pivoted on the spot and he took a couple of steps back, making a camera gesture with his finger and thumb.

"Aw, so pretty, Rue-Rue. Though I have to say I prefer you *buck* naked." His cackles increased to a full-bellied wheeze, and I took another step forward and threw out a hand.

THWACK!

Que fell backwards, straight onto his tight little ass, holding his cheek while his glare bounced between me and the dead fish in my grip.

"Not so funny now, huh?" I asked from where I was towering above him, unable to stop my own laughter.

Que stared up at me, challenge dancing in his beautiful blue eyes, and I smirked back at him.

"Do I need to shove Christmas lights up your ass too?" I warned with a low chuckle.

His grin was wicked. "It's not lights I want you to shove inside my asshole, Rue-Rue."

I shook my head, smiling to myself when he sat up, tugged at my jumpsuit, and started to reach inside my underwear for exactly what he wanted *inside that ass.*

PLOOF!

What. The. Fuck.

I reached a hand to the back of the deer skull still mounted on my head and felt the melting snow before turning around to seek out its origin. It took me a second to find her when she darted back behind a tree, but there was no hiding the mop of red hair blowing in the wind.

The little shit peeked her head out and I spotted the

ice balls loaded in her arms. She was bare-assed, her skin almost as white as the snow, in nothing but an apron and a pair of bulky boots that were way too big for her.

"Spreadin' holiday cheer, boys?" she called out to us, and I narrowed my glare at her. My dick as hard as it was before, but now with a new target in mind. This girl needed to be taught a lesson that was slightly less forgiving than a tail of Christmas lights.

Que looked at me, and I nodded towards the pile of bones on the ground. He smirked and followed my unspoken directions, placing the second skull onto his head before cracking his neck.

Nickie eyed us with curiosity and excitement, her jittery figure bouncing up and down in the distance. "Aw, it's my wittle reindeer! What toys can I get from your sacks?"

She giggled and twirled around like a deranged fucking moron, and I growled, gripping Que by the wrist and stalking towards her, shoulder to shoulder.

"Better run now, little girl. Because when we catch you, we're going to rip your insides the fuck open."

CHAPTER 20
NICKIE

Something about this felt familiar. Me running through the woods, covered in blood.

I shook the thought from my head and ran faster. It wasn't exactly fair that I was so much smaller or that the trail of blood would lead them right to me.

I tried to quiet my heavy breathing, not particularly sure if Soda Pop meant to rip me open like I enjoyed or rip me open like one of Dahmer's houseguests. Either way, I needed to get somewhere they wouldn't find me.

Outsmarting these two wasn't gonna be easy, but that's what had my pussy absolutely clenching. I could still feel a little piece of the bulb in my back door, and that gave me a tiny bolt of energy to keep moving.

They'd be able to sniff me out in no time if I stayed in the woods, so instead, I doubled-back to where I'd found them making out by the lake. Using the sound of the rushing water to cover my tracks as I laid down and hid next to one of the piles of deer meat.

"Ew, you two stink," I said, waving a hand over my nose. Apparently dead things stunk.

Was that a size kinda situation or was it all dead things? I wondered to myself.

For hunters, the boys were not very quiet. I could hear them cracking sticks under their giant feet, and I couldn't help but giggle.

"Hey, did ya hear that, Rue-Rue? Looks like Red wants to play hide and seek."

"Oh no, he's gonna find us, Bambi!" I squealed.

Bambi didn't reply, though. He was taking an open-eyed nap when I was in dire need of some assistance.

"So desperate for that loose cunt to be filled you didn't bother to run?" Soda Pop added.

I could sense them behind me, getting closer and closer by the second.

"We see you, you little shit."

I peeked over the deer's torso and I saw them too. Their onesies were tied around their waists like Blitzy had done with his, abs for fucking days both shining in the sunlight.

"You better watch out. You better not hide..." Que said, tilting his head as he crouched down in front of me, the deer skull following along with his movements. I blinked when something wet dripped off its nose and splattered onto the snow. More blood. "You better keep quiet, I'm telling you why..."

I knew that song but Rabbit Man was getting the words all wrong.

I swallowed, watching Soda Pop's eyes darken behind the slits in his deer skull mask. "'Cause we're gonna take you fucking down."

Those were definitely the wrong words but I didn't have time to think about that now.

I whimpered, backing up but going nowhere with the big carcasses piled around me. Que lifted me up as easy as a feather and held me out towards his partner in crime.

"Open your fucking mouth and get my dick wet for your sake," Rudy said, pulling his massive cock free of his squeaky jumpsuit.

"I'd listen if I were you. You're awfully heavy. Wouldn't want you to slip..." Que added, pretending to drop me, only to yank me back up at the last second.

I frowned. I didn't like the idea of falling so I did exactly as I was told and opened my mouth as wide as it would go.

Que propped the deer skull on the tippy top of his head, flipped me around like a rag doll, and shoved my pussy into his face while lowering mine onto Rudy's cock. "All the better to eat you with, Red." He chuckled against my clit, and I whimpered when Rudy plowed as far back as my throat would allow him.

Blood. Saliva. And fucking come. That's all I was to them. All I became as Que licked at my pussy at the same time Rudy destroyed my mouth.

"That's enough. This isn't a reward. Set her down, Thumper," Soda Pop grunted.

Que pulled back and I whined, kicking my feet and trying to get back to that delicious tongue of his. It was no use. He set me down on my feet and yanked at the string to my apron. It fluttered in the breeze and landed in a pile on the snow.

"That's better," he said, flicking my nipples and making them pucker even more. Rudy was staring at my ass. A low chuckle rumbled his chest, and I frowned before glancing over a shoulder to follow his line of sight.

"Why am I even surprised?" he said, plucking up a small green cable and pulling until I could hear a *pop, pop, pop* sound coming from behind me.

I'd forgotten about those.

Rudy shook his head at me, shoving a section of Christmas lights against my mouth and wrapping them around and around my head. All that was missing was an apple.

"Hehe! Oink. Oink," I mumbled around the cable as it dug into the corners of my lips.

"Shut up and bend over. You've been a bad girl, Nickie, and need a lesson in obedience. One that you apparently haven't fucking learned yet," Rudy grumbled, and I felt the shivers again but this time it was because his fingers were poking at my ass.

Que stroked Rudy's cock a few times before pulling away, and I hissed when Rudy's hand plowed into my rear while Que rammed his against my pussy.

"High-fiving inside me, boys?"

"Keep talking and I'll high-five your face."

Que snickered, dropping his arm and positioning himself behind me. "Looks like we finally found a way to shut her up."

"Nah. She'll be screaming in a minute," Rudy replied, as his dick inched at my rear hole.

"Oh, fucking hell, that's hot," Que groaned in approval, someone's palms on each of my cheeks. Spreading me wider. "Better make room, Red. You're not full yet."

My eyes widened, and I barely had time to breathe before I felt Que's cock pushing in alongside Rudy's, trying to rut into my hole while the rest of me was breaking in two. "Ah—fuck! Yes, more!"

The boys grunted, adjusting themselves until they found a rhythm that had them both fucking up inside me.

"Oh fuck, Red, you're taking us so fucking well," Que whispered, and I melted against him. I wanted to be a good girl most of the time. Sometimes I just did bad things. "Keep it up. Milk our cocks. Make us come for you."

"Nah. She can handle more. Let's hear you scream for it. For us," Rudy chimed in. "Scream for our come—fucking earn us emptying into this pathetic hole."

I couldn't breathe. One guy praising me while the other degraded me. Like being stuck between hot and cold until the two met in the middle and everything went warm.

"Fuck! I'm coming! Fuck yes, Red. Feel the way I fill that tight ass!"

Rudy moaned louder when Que was mid-nut, and the fire inside my bum was quickly cooled by a splash of thick come.

"Your turn, Soda Pop!" I barely got the words out before Rudy was bending me in half and pounding me harder.

Que must have tugged himself free already because a few seconds later he was standing in front of me, shoving his semi-limp dick into my mouth and instructing me to suck it clean. "Give it to her, baby," he crooned. "Let me watch you fucking break her."

That did it. Rudy burst inside me, his dick popping off just like a soda bottle when you shake it. I could feel every spurt of his orgasm, and I smiled.

"On your fucking knees for me. Now," he barked, and I tipped forward, my palms spread out in the snow. I could barely stand anyway.

Rudy grabbed me around the torso and tugged me back upright. "Uh-uh. Not you."

"A gift for mwah?" Que mocked. "Have I been a good boy? You sure I deserve it?" He chuckled as he did exactly like he was told.

All the blood drained from my face when I watched Que positioned himself between my legs again, Broody Rudy's ominous shadow standing behind him.

Were they gonna...

"Lick every last drop, Thumper," Rudy demanded, and Que buried his mouth against my ass, his tongue licking inside and out. Till nothing was left but a wet streak of saliva.

He moaned, and at first, I thought he was just really enjoying his treat. But then I felt myself being *thumped* forward, and I realized Rudy wasn't just behind Que. He was inside him.

"Oh, holy fucking hell," I groaned while Que whimpered.

"Right there, fuck! You sure know how to destroy someone's ass—"

Rabbit Man's words were cut short when Rudy started fucking him harder, and I fell face-first into the snow with the force.

Rudy laughed, pausing his brutal pounding just long enough to set me back up on all fours. And then he was at it again.

My pussy was weeping. I was so turned on I couldn't breathe. I couldn't move. I was crying out to the devil and singing up to the angels. Until Que gripped my hips and situated himself on top of my back, bracing his body weight with one foot on each side of me. Rudy hummed in approval, forcing Rabbit Man's cock to slide into my drenched cunt with a slow precision.

"Stuff my stocking, boys!" I hollered over a shoulder, and Rudy grunted, "If she's talking, you aren't doing a good enough job to earn my cock back inside that tight little ass."

Que shut me up real quick after that, pounding the fuck out of me. Guess that was why they called him *Thumper*. He fucked so fast I couldn't keep track of my hands scrambling beneath us.

"Ah! Yes, just like that!" Rudy was back inside Que now, while I got to enjoy the ride of my life, my limp body sliding back and forth on the snow.

My ears were ringing, my boys were singing, and balls were swinging in this winter wonderland.

CHAPTER 21
QUE

"You can put 'er down, you know." I looked over to where Nickie was bouncing off Rudy's shoulder each time he took a step in the knee-high snow.

He didn't respond, just set her onto her feet. She sprinted to the left. He took three more large steps, scooped her up around her waist, and slung her back over a shoulder again. Then he turned to me and cocked an eyebrow.

"Right, point made. Ya don't have to be smug about it," I grumbled.

"You're one to talk," he threw back at me, and now I was the one grinning. Not because the fucker was right but because of what he was being right about.

Five years together plus the other four before that meant I didn't need him to say a word for me to know what the big guy was thinking. His little mannerisms said it all. The tightening of his jaw muscle, the twitching of his lips, the crinkling of the lines around his eyes he'd swear he didn't have.

Don't let 'em fool ya. Broody Rudy was just as vain as I was. He was just better at hiding it from everyone who wasn't me.

It was why I'd waited and watched, never pushing him for more until the time was right. Was I flirty? Did I hint at it? 'Course. Would have been weird if I hadn't. But I never pushed the stubborn bastard. Just his buttons. In every other sense, I'd been patient. Wined and dined him —toilet wine and rations I'd stolen outta the prison commissary. But beggars couldn't be choosers.

Point was, our connection went deeper than the physical and the physical went small-intestine *deep*. Still, the first time he let me kiss him on the mouth was deeper than that...

"Weber, Laurent, kitchen duty. Now!" Officer O'Reilly barked out from the other side of the bars.

I looked to Rudy, who looked back over at me. His way of telling me to shut my trap. I smirked. My way of telling him there wasn't a chance in hell of that happening.

I stepped up to the bars and slipped my arms through the little slot in the door, waiting to be cuffed. "Thought Kelly and Mitchel were on kitchen duty this week?" I asked, brushing O'Reilly's wrist with my thumb as he dropped my bracelets in place and cinched 'em extra tight. "You wouldn't be playing favorites, now would ya, officer?"

"That mouth is gonna get you in trouble one of these days, inmate," he grunted under his breath.

"Good thing it gets me outta trouble too." I winked at him, my eyes flicking down to the stiffy I could make out in O'Reilly's uniform pants.

"Knock it off, Laurent," he hissed.

"Got it, boss." I stepped back and offered him a mock salute that looked about as weird as it felt with my hands joined at the wrists.

Rudy stepped up to the door next, the process much quicker for someone whose favorite pastime wasn't talking back.

A few minutes later, we were walking out of B-Block, past several more security doors, and deposited into the kitchen area. Then O'Reilly released our wrists and slammed the door shut.

"You got twenty minutes, Laurent," he whispered from the other side while Rudy crossed his arms and glared at me.

"What's going on?"

I shrugged a shoulder before disappearing into the walk-in fridge. Reappearing with a few Twinkies pushed together to look like a cake, a shit-ton of Cool Whip globbed on top, and two little figures made from toothpicks sticking out.

"And what is that supposed to be?" he asked. Mostly because he was looking for something to say. We both knew what today was. What it was supposed to be. We both also didn't talk about it, even though I thought we should.

"It's no designer wedding cake, but it was the best I could do considering the circumstances." I kept my eyes focused on his, even as he was shooting daggers into my forehead.

"Don't..."

"Why not?" I turned my back on him and used some dental floss I'd pinched to cut the cake into slices. The knives were all behind locked doors, and it would take more than a quick blowie for O'Reilly to agree to that one. He'd already given me two visits to Rudy's cell this month alone—codefendants weren't supposed to CO-mingle.

I slopped a piece of Twinkie cake onto a plate and passed it to Rudy while he continued to stare at it like it might eat him instead. "I'm not doing this, Que."

"Yes, you are," I replied simply. "I think instead of moping around all day, we should celebrate."

"Celebrate what?" I could see the way his jaw was ticking. Most people would assume he was angry. He wasn't. He was hurting. Worse than I'd ever seen him hurt before. "The fact she cheated on me? The fact I lost my mind? The fact I killed her?"

"The fact you dodged a bullet... and she didn't." I shook my head, plucking a piece of cake off the counter and smashing it into his face.

Rudy just continued to stare at me for a moment, Cool Whip dripping off his chin and little bits of Twinkie clinging to the inside of his nose. Beneath it, his skin was turning red while the vein on the side of his neck was pulsing. "I can't believe you just did that..."

"Whelp, believe it." I swiped up a dollop of cream from the tip of his nose with my index finger and sucked it clean. Nearly biting it off when Rudy smashed his own piece of cake into the side of my head when I wasn't looking. I turned back and grinned at him. "If you wanted to give me a facial, Rue-Rue, all ya had to do was ask."

He shook his head disapprovingly, but he was grinning. Or almost grinning. His lip was a little higher on one side at the very least. Higher than that when I took another piece of cake and chucked it at his chest. And then we were laid out, flat on our backs on the kitchen floor, covered in Cool Whip and Twinkie icing while staring up at the drop ceiling.

After a few minutes of silence, Rudy sighed, his voice barely a whisper when he said, "Thanks."

I rolled onto an elbow to look at him while he continued to avoid looking at me. "Close your eyes," I told him.

"What?"

"You heard me, asshole. Close your eyes," I repeated.

"Why? What are you gonna do?" he side-eyed me.

"If I wanted to ravage your ass, it wouldn't be all that hard to do when you're sleeping. Now be a good boy and close your eyes, Weber."

He huffed and puffed, but after a few more seconds, he closed his eyes and I lowered my mouth to his, brushing lightly at first. Then deepening it when he didn't instantly curse me out or pull away. It didn't take long after that for him to let me shove my tongue down his throat. I climbed on top of him, straddling his torso as he gripped me around the waist.

He wouldn't open his eyes, though. Just like I knew he wouldn't, not until he accepted it was finally okay for him to move on. Even if that moving on was with another dude.

"I could toss your ass across the room if I wanted to, ya know," Rudy grumbled from beneath me.

"You don't want to."

"Yeah, and how do you know?"

"'Cause right now your dick is poking me in the dick." I grinned. "Besides, every groom deserves to get kissed on his wedding day," I whispered at the same time O'Reilly started pounding on the kitchen door, signaling that our time was up.

Another few more loud, quick taps broke me out of that memory and had me staring at the cabin door. Blitz tugged it open with a joint pressed between his lips and a cookie he must have saved in a hand.

Rudy stalked past him and dropped Nickie onto the couch a little rougher than necessary. "I don't care what you do with her, but don't you dare let her out of your sight—and I mean it..."

He gave Dane and Dash a pointed look. The fear of the unknown was much worse than anything he could have said as he stomped to the back of the cabin. I followed him, stopping short when he started dragging a little sled back up the hill towards our drop site.

"Pick up the pace, Thumper! Or do I have to carry your ass too?" he yelled out, and I grinned.

"Wouldn't mind a little princess treatment if I'm being honest," I yelled back.

CHAPTER 22
NICKIE

I waited until the cabin door slammed shut to roll off Granny's couch and jump to my feet. Blitz immediately stepped in front of the now-closed door while Dane blocked the hallway and Vix barricaded the basement.

"Boooo, you guys are no fun," I whined, crossing my arms over my chest and stomping a foot.

"Hey! Those are mine!" Dash shouted, moving around the kitchen island. Shoving my ass back down on the couch and swiping his boots off my feet.

"Ow," I grumbled and rubbed at my backside, rolling off the seat cushion again and landing on my knees in front of the sofa. My upper body propped up and my ass popped out. "I'll trade ya for 'em." I fluttered my lashes at Dash over a shoulder, while gesturing to my leaky asshole.

He shook his head. "Uh, no thanks. I'm not really into... ass play."

"Liar!" Dane called out from the hallway.

"Shut up," Dash called back.

"I don't want ya to fuck me, dumb-dumb," I sighed before adding, "Well, not right now. I want ya to remove the piece of glass. Be a dear, would ya?"

That was something Granny always used to say. *Be a dear…*

Guess I was starting to miss her more than I thought I would. The whole *you don't know whatcha got till it's gone* thing. I had different kinds of deer now.

Dash stood up and nodded to Dane, who disappeared down the hallway. The bathroom door opened, and a few seconds later, it closed again and Dane came strolling around the corner with a pair of tweezers in hand. He passed them to Dash, who squatted behind me. One palm leaning on the small of my back, the other sliding between the crack in my cheeks.

He snapped his fingers at Vix, who mumbled under his breath before removing a flask from his front pocket and handing it to Dash.

"I'm gonna need to sterilize the wound first," he said to me. I could hear him pour some of the liquor onto the tweezers. It splattered onto my toes too.

"What's that supposed to mean?" I asked him.

"It means this *is* gonna hurt, sweetheart," Dane shouted from where he reposted himself up by the hallway.

"Don't listen to him. He's just tryin' to scare you," Dash whispered. "But he's probably right. It ain't gonna feel nice."

"I'm not afraid of a little pain." I shrugged, grabbing onto the couch cushion and clenching tight.

Dash slapped my ass cheek. "Relax or it's gonna go deeper."

"Oooo, I like it deeper." I giggled and earned myself another swat.

"Not in your rectum, you don't," he grunted.

"Rectum," I repeated and giggled more. "That's an awfully big word for you, ain't it? What are you some sorta doctor or something?"

Dash's eyes flicked up to where I was still peering over a shoulder before dropping to where he had my ass cheeks spread wide in front of him.

"Like whatcha see, Doc?" I wiggled my eyebrows up and down, wincing when the alcohol splashed my skin. Leaving a trail of liquid fire from the top of my asshole down to my pussy lips.

Ouch! That shit burned. Someone was gonna have to lick it up and kiss it better now.

"Not a doctor." He waited for me to stop wiggling, then pressed a hand down on my back again. "What's your favorite color?"

"Red—ow!" I whimpered as he tugged a chunk of glass free without warning. "Why do you care about my favorite color all of a sudden?"

"I don't. I was just tryin' to get ya to relax." Dash held the little green shard up to the light and twirled it around a few times, blood splattering onto his hand, though he didn't seem to notice or care all that much.

"'Kay, how about an EMT? Or a murse!" I continued with my probing as soon as Mr. Handsy was done with his.

"A murse?"

I flipped back around, dragging my blood-covered ass onto Granny's sofa without much thought. It wasn't like she could yell at me now. "A male nurse," I clarified. "A murse."

"A male nurse is just called a nurse." Dash pushed up on the coffee table and rose to his full height. Then he tipped his head to one side to look at me, like I was stupid. I wasn't stupid. I was just... spirited. That's what all the doctors in the white coats used to say.

The girl is spirited. It didn't hurt that I'd suck their cocks as soon as the exam room doors closed. That was smart, if you asked me. Keeping all the doctors in your pocket so they didn't tell your daddy you were crazy.

"Whatever." I rolled my eyes. "So you're a male nurse, then?"

Dash paused to look at someone standing behind me before answering. "I worked in a prison hospital. Decided it wasn't for me."

One of the twins walked over and slapped Dash upside the back of the head.

"Ow, what?" he grunted. "She isn't gonna say anything to anyone."

I shimmied up higher on the sofa, tucking my legs to my chest and covering my knees with Granny's apron. I always did love a good story time. "So?" I urged him.

"So what?" Dash asked me.

"Why wasn't it for you?"

He lifted a nonchalant shoulder, his eyes scanning the room, then quickly dropping to his shoeless feet. "Didn't think everyone who was there belonged there is all..."

CHAPTER 23
RUDY

It didn't take long before Que's toned ass was jogging in front of me. And all I wanted now was to slam him against the tree and fuck him again...

No, Rudolph. Move your ass and get to the meat before it spoils out in the sun.

Que looked over a shoulder and smirked at me, and then another snow ball was tossed in my direction.

"Hey, what the fuck?" I ducked my head to avoid the next barrage of ice bullets. "Unless you want those balls shoved up your ass, cut the shit."

Que giggled, jogging backwards and doing a mass toss of the last pile he had left in his arms.

"Agh, you fucker! Fine, you asked for it." I didn't give him a chance to dodge. I made for a right while lunging left, rushing forward and slamming into him on the ground. He grunted and laughed harder while I huffed into his face.

"Don't be too mad, Rue-Rue. If I recall correctly,

throwing shit at you happened to be the best decision of my life."

I bristled for a moment. That memory in the prison's kitchen flashing back to me like slides on a projector screen. The kiss. The first time I let myself feel something that wasn't anger and resentment over fucking Holly. I didn't know what my life would have looked like if I hadn't pulled the trigger. But now, staring down at Que's beautiful blue eyes and carefree smile made me realize...

I'd do it again. Just to be here. With him.

"Close your eyes, Quentin," I whispered, leaning down and grazing his lips with mine.

His breath caught in his throat and he obeyed, albeit slowly, his mouth slightly parted, waiting for me to recreate that memory.

I did kiss him, deep and with my whole fucking soul, but when he started grinding on my dick, making me forget our reason for being out here, I gripped a handful of slush in my hand and smashed it into Que's beautifully smug face.

He didn't move, just stared up at the sky, and blinked. Then I rolled off him in a fit of laughter I couldn't contain. I laughed so hard and for so long that chill penetrating my clothes hit my balls and I hissed at the icy burn.

"C'mon, Thump. I'll fill your fucking hole later. We need to get back before dark," I finally said, the laughter bubbling to the surface all over again when he pushed himself up and glared at me.

"Funny. That's not how I remember that night going," he grumbled as I yanked him to his feet and we kept trudging towards the lake with the sled in tow.

Once we hit the water's edge, I got to work, grabbing

the bucks by the legs and dragging their bodies over. The meat we'd carved was still spread out on a rock, dusted on top with some snow and a bit of dirt.

"What are you doing?" Que called after me when I grabbed the meat and made my way to the embankment.

"Gotta clean these before we can cook 'em," I explained, sticking my hands into the freezing water and rinsing off the chunk of deer.

Que winced, likely seeing how my skin turned bright red from the frigid temperatures.

"Listen, I like your hands too much for you to lose them to frostbite," he whined, skipping small rocks across to the deep end of the lake. "I wonder if this thing is natural or manmade—"

THUNK!

Que froze and looked over at me. But I wasn't moving either. Just staring out at the water while trying to wrap my head around the source of the sound.

"The fuck? That ain't no fish. Something big is down there," he said.

Instead of replying to the obvious, I shook my hands in the water, watching the ripples distort the reflection in the waves. There was definitely something there.

"What do you think it is?" I said, more to myself, pushing to my feet and walking around to the other side. I needed to get closer without actually taking an ice bath.

"The Loch Ness Monster—wait, never mind, that's in your pants!" Que cackled while following at my heels. It was a stupid joke. It was also something he did whenever he was anxious. He'd try to make light of a situation by tossing humor at it.

Rolling my eyes, I snatched up some more rocks and took aim.

THUNK.

THUNK.

THUNK.

"It's fucking heavy." I assessed the sounds, continuing to chuck little pebbles and stones around the object to gauge how big it was and what shape it might have been.

"What is it, Rue-Rue?" Que questioned, his eyes following each rock as I tossed it out in front of us.

"I don't know yet." I scooped up another pile and balanced myself on the edge of the muddy snow surrounding the bank.

"Want me to jump in to look?" he continued, and I sighed.

"No. I'd prefer your dick didn't become a popsicle, thanks."

Que snickered. "Aw, you do love me."

I scoffed but couldn't help the smile playing on my lips. Maybe I did. Who the fuck knew?

Those words were easy for Que to say and he said them often. Me, not so much. Didn't mean I didn't feel deeply for the guy. I just didn't know what I felt. Falling in love with my best friend was not how I saw my future playing out. Neither was a life sentence, though.

"Maybe Nickie knows what's down there?"

Hmm. It was possible. Or her grandmother—wherever the fuck she went.

"I don't think she would tell us," I countered.

Que just shrugged. "Guess we all have our secrets. She doesn't exactly know she's sharing her home with a bunch of escaped convicts."

I shook my head. *No, secrets were not safe.* We needed to know what was down there.

I sighed, turning and walking back towards the sled. I placed the tugline on the palm of Que's hand. "Go back and give the meat to the guys."

He smiled. I could see the smart-ass remark burning the tip of his tongue. But instead of saying something like "oh, I'll give them the meat" or whatever other nonsense he usually came up with, he gave me a quick peck and started to walk away.

I stopped him with a hand on his shoulder. "And... bring that little shit back here with you."

CHAPTER 24
NICKIE

Just as I was about to give Dash a proper blowie as a thank you for fixing my asshole, Que was smacking the door wide open, all puffed up and ruffled with snow.

"Where's Nickie?" I heard him call from the back door. The other guys tattled on me in five seconds flat.

"Damn it, boys! Don't be rats. Rats get snapped," I grumbled, popping out from under Granny's stinky old blanket she'd knitted herself before pulling it over my head again. Maybe she had some mouse traps around here too.

"Nickie. Come on. The big man needs you." Que sighed.

My ears perked up, and I sprang to my feet, swatting Dash's bobbing dick out of my way to look over at Que. "Soda Pop needs me? For what?"

"Looks like you can melt even Mr. Freeze's ice-cold heart." Blitz chuckled as I padded over to the blonde-haired hunk still dripping wet with snow.

I wonder what kinda other fluids he had dripping on him?

Que finished clearing the piles of meat off the sled and instructed the rest of the guys to put it away in Granny's storage freezer.

"Boys, you're not getting out of dinner! I'll be right back. Start the brownies while I'm gone, okay?"

The twins winked at me, Dash grumbled to himself and tugged the blanket back over his head, Dane just laughed at him, Vix tipped his bottle, and Blitz blew a smoke ring in my direction.

"Sir, yes, sir!" I said to Que, accepting the coat he was offering to me. It smelled like mothballs and old people.

Then he picked up the flashlight and pocketed it before draping another jacket across his arms. Those ones belonged to Grandaddy I think. Granny never talked about him anymore. I was pretty sure it made her sad.

"At attention, soldier?" I rubbed up against Que and the flagpole poking me through his onesie, but he just groaned and twirled me in front of him, bopping my sore ass and ushering me out the door.

It was colder than before since the sun was getting lower in the sky, but we could see well enough with the flashlight guiding the way and the sled bouncing behind us.

"We're here, Rue-Rue! Where you at?" Que shouted, walking a few steps in front of me while I checked out our surroundings.

We were back by the lake. *Just keep swimming, swimming, swimming.*

"Hey, Nickie. We found something." Rudy said, accepting the coat Que shoved onto his shoulders as he approached.

"Something?" I repeated, my wide eyes bouncing

around the woods. I hoped those wolves he mentioned weren't anywhere nearby. "What something?"

The boys stepped towards me, and I watched the snow collect in their hair. One dark and one light.

"Yes. Something," Que said. "We were hoping you'd be able to tell us about it."

I followed their line of sight as their gazes swept towards the lake, and I shivered. "Uh, the Loch Ness Monster?"

"That's what I said!" Que slapped the back of a hand against his friend's chest and we laughed together until Soda Pop cleared his throat.

"This is serious. There's a very large object submerged in the deep end of the lake. I can't get to it. Do you know anything about what might be down there?"

Just keep swimming.

"A lot could be floating in a lake, Prudey Rudy." I shrugged, the chill continuing to travel up and down my spine as the snow pelted my head.

"Do you know anything about it? Anything at all that could help, Red? Rudy thinks it's something bad. Do you remember anyone throwing something down there? Your grandmother maybe?"

"Gran isn't down there! I swear, silly gooses." I shook my head and chuckled.

The boys looked at each other and then back at me. "Okay... I meant did your grandmother throw something in the lake..." Que tried again, pausing before adding, "Where *is* your grandmother, Nickie?"

I chewed on my bottom lip, the sour memory resurfacing in my brain until it popped like bubble wrap. "She's no longer with us," I stated primly, copying what my daddy said when my sister was knocked over the head with a hatchet.

They shared another look. "So... your grandmother left you the cabin?" Que said, quiet and soft like.

"Yep. It's all mine now."

"Copy that. Thanks." Rudy scratched the scruff on his chin and peered over at the lake before nodding to me. "You can head back. Que and I will grab the rest of the supplies and meet you there, okay?"

Just keep swimming.

I winked. "You got it, Soda Pop! Don't be late because we're preparin' a feast! Last one there gets intestines and butt flanks!"

Que and Rudy gave me matching smiles, and I skipped away.

Back to my cabin. Back to my toys. Back to my delicious roundup of boys.

CHAPTER 25
QUE

Rudy parked the sled with the last of the meat next to the front door with a grunt, while I came up behind him with a sack of fish slung over my shoulder like Santa Claus.

"Merry fucking Christmas!" I sang out as I dropped the sack onto the landing and nudged Rudy with an elbow. All I got was a side-eye in return. "Lighten up, will ya? We are breathing in fresh air, having more sex than is good for us, *and*..." I gestured to the cabin window. "Looks like the power came back on. What more could ya ask for?"

Rudy shook his head and rubbed at the back of his neck. "I don't know. Something just doesn't feel right, Thumper."

"It's cause of Prat, ain't it?" I swatted Rudy's hand away and pressed my fingers into the muscles giving him trouble. "Maybe he saw his chance to make a run for it and he took it? Can't fault the guy if he did. Lots of guys would do the same."

"Yeah, just didn't take him for one of them. Especially

after all this time. Why wait until we were already running? Why ditch us now? After we had a plan? Sure, it got a little fucked I guess but..."

I shrugged, the cold rush of being out all day finally catching up to me and sending a chill up my spine. My stomach was rumbling too as phantom smells carried their way into my nose. It was like we were back home at my aunt's place while my ma had her stew simmering on the stove. I could practically taste the meat and potatoes.

"Easier for one guy to get away in a car than risk a group of us getting caught on foot," I said.

"Yeah, maybe." Rudy pried my fingers off the back of his neck and twisted my wrist until I was standing in front of him. He dropped it and then gave me a quick swat on the ass, ushering me closer to the cabin like I had done a few hours ago when I'd been trying to rush Nickie out of it.

This outdoorsy shit was good for the big guy. Made him more playful than I'd seen him in ages.

I twisted the knob and shoved my way through the door, pausing in my tracks with Rudy stopping short behind me.

The whole place looked like a regurgitated Hallmark movie with twinkling lights strung over the fireplace and extending to that lopsided shrub of tree in the corner, a miniature Christmas village spread out on the coffee table, and decorative pillows on every soft surface.

I looked to Dane, who just shrugged, and then back over to Dash. "He said not to let her out of our sights. We figured it was better to let her do her thing. It wasn't like the place couldn't use a little sprucing up. Besides, I think it looks nice."

Nickie turned from where she was fussing around on the stove and smiled at his praise. Not the off-the-hinges smile I was used to seeing on her when she was getting under your skin, or more often than not, putting her mouth on it. But a soft smile, and it gave me the same kinda warm feeling I got whenever I could get Rudy to smile for real too.

Don't get me wrong. I didn't love the girl. Not like I loved him. Loved fucking her, sure. Loved her fucking me even more. But she was starting to grow on me.

I glanced over to Rudy and noticed a strange look on his face. I think she was starting to grow on him too. He liked the challenge. He also liked the chase. Fucker would never admit it, but he couldn't deny that this was *nice*. Having most of us in one place on Christmas Eve, the fire going and more food than we had seen in ages. I listened to the hum of the radio while some staticy holiday music played in the background until it was abruptly cut off by a news report.

"Be on the lookout for convicted kill—"

Nickie quickly switched the station.

"Escaped—"

She switched it one more time and then a soft Christmas carol was playing again.

"I made dinner!" she announced, practically bouncing up and down on her heels with excitement.

I looked to Rudy. He shook his head. His way of telling me not to react. Then I peered back into the kitchen.

Red seemed to be none the wiser. She also seemed super content. She'd thrown on an old dress—probably something she took out of her granny's closet—that she'd cinched around the waist with what appeared to be a piece of shoelace and tied her red hair high up on her head.

"Does it have any drugs in it? I don't feel like being sleep-fucked again," Rudy grunted, tugging his boots off and setting them out by the fireplace to dry.

Nickie lifted a hand from the pot she was stirring and gestured with her thumb and index finger. "*Maybe* a little bit... but only in the brownies."

Rudy shot her another glare from where he'd spread himself out across the couch.

"Scout's honor!" She lifted two fingers into a peace sign.

And Dash chimed in, "I watched her make 'em. Everything is safe but the brownies."

"Perfectly safe for me," Blitz added as he plucked a brownie from the top of the pile and stuck two more into his pockets. "I'll take Rudy's if he doesn't want 'em."

"I'm sure ya will," Rudy grumbled, and I walked over and cracked him on the head.

"Be nice," I muttered under my breath. "And say thank you to Red for cooking for us."

He narrowed his eyes at me, and I narrowed mine right back while crossing my arms over my chest. "Not everyone finds your assholishness as charming as I do, ya know."

"Don't they?" He grinned, though it looked more like an upside down scowl.

I pointed around the room, and everyone responded with a "no" in some form or another before my finger finally landed on Nickie.

"Sometimes it's really mean," she said while staring at him with big green, tear-filled eyes.

"Seriously?" Rudy grunted.

"Seriously," I repeated.

"Fine!" He tugged at his collar and cleared his throat. "Thank you, ya little shit."

"For?" I pressed him and got myself another dirty look.

"*For*... making us dinner," he huffed. "There? You fucking happy?"

"Ecstatic!" I clapped my hands together and turned around to eye the table and counter full of all sorts of side dishes with some mystery meat on the platter in the middle. Honestly didn't care what it was, because it all smelled delicious. "Now let's fucking eat!"

The boys were all real grateful to have their bellies full. And I was grateful for the eye candy. There was just something so warm and tingly about watching a bunch of guys chow down on your meat.

Once everyone was done stuffing their faces, Dash jumped on dish duty while I pulled Granny's Bingo markers off the shelf in her knitting room and carried the basket back out into the living area.

"Time for reindeer games!" I yelled as I dumped the markers onto the counter, watching as a few dropped off the ledge and rolled under the stove. *Oops.*

When no one started moving, I fluttered my lashes at Que, who fluttered his at Rudy.

"Everyone up," Soda Pop barked out.

I then stamped each of their hands with a different color marker. Except for the twins. They both got green because I still couldn't tell the fuckers apart anyway. Even their dicks looked the same.

"Now what?" Dane asked while Con and Don were using two of the markers like light sabers.

"Now we play!" I clapped my hands and jumped up and down on the spot. This was going to be so much fun!

"How?" Que said as he stared down at the yellow dot on his hand. "What are the rules, Red?"

I brought a finger up to my chin and tapped on the side of my cheek a few times, trying to think of the best way to explain it before it finally came to me. "It's kinda like Twister. Left hand, red. Right foot, blue."

"'Cept we don't have one of those spinner things or a plastic mat with the circles," he replied.

"We don't need a spinny thing and I'm the board, silly. Here, let me show you." I grabbed on to Que's hand and tugged him farther into the living room. Then I took a yellow marker and dotted myself on the mouth. "That means you can put whatever part of *you* you'd like on, around, or *in...* here."

Que grinned and started pulling on the waistband of his pants. I grinned wider and dropped to my knees in front of him, sucking his cock down like a piece of spaghetti as soon as it plopped free. I gave it a few long licks before popping up and turning back towards the rest of the guys.

"See? Easy!"

"Easy as a cream pie," Que added, still stroking his dick and waving Rudy over. Then he plucked the red marker out of my hand and dotted his ass, wiggling it in Rudy's direction. "Tag, you're it."

Rudy craned his neck to the side before stalking forward and pinning Que against the wall, face-first. I pouted for a moment, realizing I wasn't the board anymore.

Then again, this could be fun too...

I grabbed the rest of the markers and went around the room once more, until each boy was a work of rainbow dotted art. And by the time I was done, my body was bent over the sofa, boobies up and head down with Que's cock in my mouth while Rudy pounded his ass from behind him. Each of the twins had their twin cocks sliding in and out of my vag at a V-shaped angle while Dane destroyed all the repair work Dash had done to my asshole.

I waved Vix over with my left hand and Blitz over with my right, matching up the colors I'd dotted on my palms and started jerking them off like Granny used to milk cows. That left my little *murse* friend to his lonesome in the corner. Watching us but a bit too timid to join.

I used my eyes to gesture to my bare chest, which was now dotted orange. Dash took a tentative step forward. Then another as I grinned through Que's rapid face-fucking. I moaned and Dash paused. I moaned again and that finally had him mounting my body from the couch cushions and grinding against my chest until the top of my head was practically touching the ground.

I could feel the blood rushing to my brain at the same time it was rushing everywhere else. Every part of me both on fire and soaking wet. Come spilling into my hair and onto my face, blood dripping out of my ass, and a rainbow of colors swirling together as the world around me convulsed and I convulsed a lot with it.

I was light-headed, dizzy, and numb. But I also wasn't. Because I felt it all. Each twitch, each spasm, each delicious thrust bombarding me on all sides while I hung upside down like an inverted cross. My legs propped up on the twins' shoulders the only thing keeping me from breaking my neck.

Vix and Blitz finished a literal handful of strokes apart, their limp cocks like bags of flesh in my closed palms. I let them go and grabbed on to Que's pant legs. He'd stopped fucking my face when I'd slid down the couch and was now jerking himself off, my mouth open and waiting. Three more thrusts of Rudy's cock had Rabbit Man making this a real white Christmas. The twins and Dane weren't far behind him until my Soda Pop remained the only hold out.

I locked glares with him when Que bend forward and dropped to his knees on the floor. Never breaking eye contact as he thrusted twice more. Too stubborn to throw his head back and enjoy it, while I was too stubborn to stop watching.

"Do it," I cheered him on. "Fuck his ass while I play with my pussy." I reached up a hand, even though my arms were Jello, and swirled a mixture of the boys' come around my clit. My nipples hardening all over again and my spine arching.

It didn't matter how many times I came in one sitting. My body always had one more to give.

A couple more swirls of my fingers and I felt that familiar sensation in my lower belly, my heart picking up speed and my toes curling. And that's when I heard it. Rudy grunted and groaning and filling Que's ass at the same time I came all over my sticky fingers.

"I like the way you punched my bingo card, daddy." I laughed and brought my thumb to my mouth, licking it clean. "Mmm, salty!"

CHAPTER 27
RUDY

"No man left behind? Isn't that what you always said, Weber? Why not me? Why was I left behind?"

The chilling words wrapped around me like a vise and I felt myself losing oxygen. The snow falling harder now, surrounding me. Drowning me. I was suffocating. I couldn't breathe.

"Pratzer. I'm sorry! I tried to find you. I did. I tried!" Desperation was clawing at my skin, the storm picking up and blinding me as the icy wind swirled around my legs and pulled me back towards a large body of water.

My boots hit the shore, and the bite of the cold had me choking on my tongue.

"Why'd you leave me? Was I not worth it? Is your red-headed fuck toy better than me? Don't I mean anything? It was us. The gang. All of us. All NINE of us. But you left me to die."

Prat's words vibrated in my skull as my body kept getting sucked into the vortex of the lake, the dark water swallowing me up until I couldn't see anything but blackness.

"No! Stop! I tried! I tried to find you. I couldn't get through the blizzard! I'm sorry! God damn it, I'm so sorry!"

His silhouette flickered into the abyss before a blurry image of tire tracks flashed into view. Then a set of keys floated in front of me, a light shining down on them from above.

Where was Dash's van?

I reached out a hand, trying to grab at the keys while still feeling like I couldn't breathe. I was dying. I was sure of it. Sinking into the dark depths. I couldn't escape...

"No!" I jolted awake, flinging up on the couch like a zombie. Que grumbled beside me, and I rubbed my eyes, looking at the rest of the guys spread out around us. Safe and sated. Nickie was tangled on the floor with the twins and Dane. All of them naked and covered in come.

I sighed and shook my head, my eyes catching on my reflection in one of the old lady's photos on the wall.

"What the fuck have we gotten ourselves into?" I mumbled to myself, unlinking my body from Que's and kissing him softly.

He looked peaceful. Hell, the fucker looked downright happy. Could I ever give him that? Maybe he was right and I needed to lay off the little shit and enjoy this for what it was.

Home.

The cuckoo clock on the back wall scared me half to death when it busted out and dropped a decrepit-looking bird out of the wooden block, before breaking altogether on the midnight position.

"Merry Christmas, you filthy animals," I mumbled to the sleeping forms on the ground. Then my glare landed on Nickie. "And to you too, fuckwit."

Que stirred again, opening his eyes and staring at me in

his cute, heavy-blinking state. "Why are you awake? Need me to blow you to bed?"

I snorted, patting his head and laying him back down on his makeshift pillow. "Nah, get some sleep. I gotta take a piss."

Que smiled and yawned. Then he reached out a hand, tapped my dick, and blew it a kiss. "Okey-dokey, dick so chokey."

He rolled over, and I got to my feet quickly before I was tempted to stay and watch the dumbass sleep and mumble stupid shit under his breath.

I stepped over the many limbs on the ground, my feet pausing when they got to Nickie. I glanced towards the hallway where the bathroom light was creeping around the corner and back down to her sleeping form.

You thirsty, shithead?

I pulled my dick out of my underwear and crouched down on my knees, quietly gripping Nickie's face in my hands, propping her head up and pressing her lips against my crown.

"Open wide," I grunted. "I'm giving you a sour taste of your own medicine."

Even asleep, this dumb broad knew how to suck cock. Muscle memory or some warped version of it, I guess. I felt the heat rise in my nuts, enjoying the way her silent tongue worked me over. I wasn't going to give her my come, though. Not this time. She'd had enough of it all over her already.

"Swallow, Nickie. Every drop," I warned before pissing down her throat. She choked a little before sucking it down in thick, greedy pulls like the come slut that she was.

As soon as my bladder was empty, I set her head back

down and started to stand until the puddle of piss on the floor caught my attention. Whatever Nickie hadn't managed to swallow caught in a seam of the floorboards, running down and accumulating in one spot.

I followed the stream, kneeling by the pool where the urine had collected and started dripping through the cracks with a soft *pfft* noise. I crept closer and noticed the board appeared slightly higher than the rest of them, and with a soft jiggle, it lifted.

My pulse spiked when I peered inside and realized what I was looking at. A plastic bag covered in blood. My body was vibrating, all my past training screaming at me not to touch this, reminding me about the DNA, cross contamination, and so many other protocols that had my head spinning.

But I didn't work for *them* anymore. They'd all turned their backs on me. I was on the other side of those bars now.

"Fuck it," I growled, sticking my hand into the hole and snatching the bag from beneath the floorboard. "What the fuck is your crazy ass hiding?"

I peeled back the two sides of the plastic, peering over a shoulder with the noise it made, then back down at what was rolled up inside.

Keys. A set of car keys.

I quickly shoved them into the dick pouch of my underwear and set the bag back into the hole before clicking the board in place. Then I jumped to my feet and rushed over to the couch. Tapping the cushion with a knee.

"Get up, Quentin. We need to leave. Now."

Que stirred again, instinctively grabbing my dick and trying to give it a tug.

"No, not that." I swatted his hand aside. "Get up. This is serious." I leaned over and bit down on his neck a little harder than usual.

"Ow! Vampire, what the fu—"

I clamped a palm over his mouth. "Shhh!"

He nodded and then we both looked over at the group on the ground. Nickie seemed to stir for a moment, popping up and staring straight ahead. Her eyes were open but she wasn't responsive. She chuckled in her sleep and laid back down.

"What the fuck are you doing, Rudy?" Que hissed at me, fully awake and ruffled now.

"Sorry," I mumbled, getting up and dressing myself before chucking his clothes and a coat at him. "We need to go for a walk."

He stared at me, clearly confused. But it didn't take him long to read my expression. His entire demeanor shifted and he got to his feet without another word.

A few minutes later, we were sneaking out the back door. Que ran behind me and yanked my shoulder damn near out of its socket, causing my jumpsuit to jingle.

Que paused, looking down and quirking one of his polished brows at me. "Uh, you know I love your dick and all but... why is there a jingle in your balls?"

Normally I'd laugh and make him fish for the answer. Right now, I was too on edge. Shoving a hand into my underwear, I retrieved the car fob and dangled it in front of Que's eyes. "Nickie isn't as innocent as you thought. And now I'm gonna prove it."

CHAPTER 28
NICKIE

Aloud bang on the front door startled me awake. I glanced out Granny's bay window and saw that the wind was picking up, rattling the cabin and causing branches to blow this way and that, while the chimney moaned and groaned.

I stretched out my arms and pushed up from the floor with a yawn, smacking my lips a few times when I noticed a sour taste in my mouth. Then I took a deep breath and scrunched up my face at the icky smell coming from beside me.

"Bad boys," I scolded, bopping Dane on the forehead when I spotted the yellow puddle next to him. It was seeping into the hardwood and stinking up Granny's fancy rug. If my daddy were here, he'd rub Daney's nose in it.

Dane yipped and shot up. "Where's the fire!"

"There's no fire. You had an accident." I pointed to the pee. He grumbled an apology, rolled over, and fell back to sleep. Boys were so gross.

Fine, you can stay stinky.

I shook my head, took another long breath through my nose, and caught a whiff of something else. "Oh, Gran. Ew."

I waved a hand over my face, the scent of the amazing food I prepared earlier tonight overpowered by a disgusting odor. Sighing, I got to my feet and walked by each of the guys, kissing them on the head one by one, and tucking them in with their blankets.

Hmm, guess you could say I was oddly attached to this group of misfits. They felt like everything I loved most about the holidays. Candy canes and fresh-baked cookies and Christmas movies and singing and dancing and sex *and pot*... all rolled-up in one.

"Whelp, I guess this couldn't last forever, could it, Gran?" I huffed as I padded towards the hallway, noting that the couch was missing the two lumps that had fallen asleep on top of it.

Oh where, oh where did my reindeer go?

I hummed the tune to myself, a little skip in my step when I looked over at Gran's knitting room, sighed again, and kept walking. Que and Rudy were probably holed up in there together and they didn't even think to invite me.

Rude.

I paused when I made it to the closet, rummaging around the shelves and tossing random pill bottles over my head.

"Bingo!" I giggled, popped the lid of Granny's poop medicine, and held it up to my mouth, guzzling more than half of the nasty-tasting liquid inside. Then I snatched everything I needed from the kitchen and finally made my way to the bathroom.

I dropped one of Granny's tin bowls in to the mouth of

the toilet and took a seat. After a lot of hunching over, my thighs achy and my asshole burning, the medicine finally started to get to work. My tummy grumbled like the Grinch, all kinds of decorating happening in the tin and toilet, until my prize popped free and clattered at the bottom.

"There you are!" I sang out as I scooped up the key from its brown, watery grave.

I took it with me into the shower and got us both squeaky clean before I held it out in front of me. Then I walked up to Gran's bedroom, taking one last peek down the hall over to where the boys were piled up on the floor behind me, unlocked her door, and tiptoed inside.

"Gran, you're not looking so hot, are you?"

CHAPTER 29
QUE

Rudy hooked an arm around the trunk of the tree, as we stood on the embankment that gave us the best overhead view of the lake, and held out the key fob he'd found stashed in the floorboards. He was convinced there was a car down there. I *wasn't* convinced it was a good idea to prove him right, but after running around the cabin and the area surrounding it clicking that damn fob with no results, I figured it best to let him try it here.

I grabbed on to his wrist to stop him from pressing the button that would trigger the lights, and he looked back at me over a shoulder.

There was a slim chance this would even work, seeing as we didn't know how long the car had been submerged—if there even was a car—but according to Rudy, the battery should be protected enough for the LEDs to flash on. Maybe the alarm too.

"Are you sure about this?" I asked him.

"What the fuck do you mean? Why wouldn't I be

sure?" he growled out, a puff of white air pushing past his lips and disappearing a few seconds later. There was less snow but a shit-ton more ice, and every time a breeze hit, the branches above us would jostle and send more clumps of frozen water onto our heads and shoulders.

I was shivering in my boots while Rudy had worked himself into a rage that had him stripping off his jacket and handing it to me on the walk here.

I peered down at the lake while I considered my answer. The top layer had frozen over and all we could see was more blackness underneath. Still, those stones we'd tossed in hit something. Which meant *something* was there. I just wasn't so sure I wanted to know what that something was. And I was also pretty certain it was better if Rudy didn't know either. Especially when he was just starting to act like his old self, maybe even a tad less broody...

"Because sometimes not knowing is better..." I admitted. I glanced down at my boots before bringing them up to lock eyes with him, a lump the size of the boulder we were standing on sinking into the pit of my stomach.

"Since when?" He shook me off him and turned back towards the lake. "Weren't you the one who told me finding out about Holly was for the best?"

I shook my head, even though he wasn't looking at me anymore. "That's different."

"Yeah? And why's that? Because it makes it okay for you to suck my dick?" he grunted.

Great, now he was pushing me away. It wasn't that I didn't love the back-and-forth, push-and-pull thing we had going on between us. It was just that I didn't like it during those few instances when I was trying to be serious.

"Don't be like that."

"Be like what?" he hissed. "Honest?"

"An asshole." I shoved at his shoulder, gripping up his jumpsuit and tugging him back when he almost toppled over the edge and went thick-skull first into the lake.

"Who's the asshole now?" He shook me off him again. "This is Prat, Que. He's one of us."

"And now so is Nickie."

Rudy spun around to wave a finger in my face. "She is *not* one of us."

"Only 'cause you won't let her be," I reminded him.

"If you like her so much, go suck her dick." I lifted an eyebrow at him and he added, "You know what I mean."

"It's not like that." I flicked his nose, leaning forward and kissing him when he blinked involuntarily. "You know you're the only nutjob for me." I grinned.

"I'm not a—you know what? Never mind." He stepped closer to the edge and looked down. "Point is… he woulda done it for us. He did do it for us. He went out there first. Alone. Because he trusted us to have his back and we let him down."

"We all knew the risks. We agreed—"

"I don't care what we agreed to. That's just something you say. At the end of the day, *I* said no man left behind. I promised…"

"This ain't all on you." I tried to grab for Rudy's arm one more time, and he moved it before I could reach him, leaning over as far as he could while directing the key fob at the lake and pressing the button.

The water lit up like Christmas morning, the ass of a van sticking up in the air with a license plate number we both recognized.

"That's Dash's car, isn't it?" I swallowed the lump that had traveled up to my neck now.

"Yeah, it is..." Rudy replied.

"You think... You don't think..." I cleared my throat. "You don't think he's down there, do you? I mean, maybe he thought someone was following him and ditched the car?"

Rudy turned around and narrowed his glare at me, his nostrils flaring beneath the glow of the moonlight. "Then how the fuck did the keys get in Nickie's cabin, under the floorboards, covered in someone's blood?"

"It's her grandmother's cabin."

"Right, so the old lady did it. Makes fucking sense."

"Where the fuck are you going?" I shouted after him, jogging through the snow just so I could catch up to his giant-ass strides.

"To figure out what the fuck is going on in that fucking house," he replied without looking at me, his strides just as giant and annoyed. Fucker wasn't slowing down.

"The house is that way." I pointed behind us. "Besides, it's cold as shit."

"Then go back. I'm sure you can find yourself a pair of tits that will help warm you up just fine. Obviously nothing is keeping you out here."

Fucking hell, less broody my ass. More jealous, for sure. That was honestly a nice change though. I enjoyed feeling appreciated.

I grinned, quickly dropping it before the big guy got the wrong impression. "That's not what I meant and you know it, dumbass. I'm just trying to figure out what the plan is here."

"The plan is... find the car, *check*." He jiggled the keys

in the air. "Find Prat and then find out what that little shit is hiding in that locked room of hers."

I shook my head, watching Rudy stomp away from me before glancing back towards the trail that led to the cabin.

Fuck...

CHAPTER 30
NICKIE

A FEW DAYS PRIOR

"Lizzie Borden took an axe and gave her mother forty whacks. When she saw what she had done, she gave her father forty-one..." I hummed the rhyme to myself over and over again as I remembered the way my big sister's head had cracked open like a ripe honeydew melon and splattered blood all over our bedroom floor.

My daddy wouldn't let me play with her after that. He said sissy wouldn't do much playin' with anyone any more *after that*. I told him she shouldn't have taken my favorite dress then.

Noelle was always stealing my things and never givin' them back. I let her keep my dress, though. I didn't want it with all the blood on it anymore anyway. What I did want was someone to play with, instead of being cooped up in this room on my lonesome.

I huffed out an annoyed breath. I was *boooooored*.

Things were quiet over on this side of the building tonight, which told me things weren't so quiet on the other side. I dropped the few kiddie books they let me keep in my room onto a pile on the floor and stepped on top to get a little peeky peek out the bulletproof window. The halls were empty, and a few seconds later, I heard the code called out over the PA system. There was a medical emergency in the main building. Which meant all the nosey Nancys were rushing over there to scope it out.

No fair! I wanted to know what was going on too, so I did that thing where I started slamming my head against the wall and making those sounds sissy made when I tried to pull the hatchet out of her skull. It had gotten stuck and I'd gotten blood all over my Mary Janes when I tried to hold her down with a foot on her chest.

Daddy hadn't liked me doing that very much. He liked it less when the doctors told him there was nothing wrong with me. Wasn't his fault, though. He didn't know I liked to play games with the doctors too.

It didn't take long for the guys at the desk to come rushing towards my room. Picking me up off the floor, dropping me onto a gurney, and wheeling me down the hall to the medical ward. I pretended to be asleep and all the people in the scrubs were too distracted by whatever was happening in one of the bays to pay much mind to me.

I peeked an eye open and then the other, before peering down at the straps on my wrists and ankles. Then I popped my thumb out of its socket and slipped an arm free, quickly unstrapping the other arm and then both my legs.

Everyone was shouting, calling out words like "emergency transport" and "extenuating circumstances." I didn't like big words. People just used 'em when they were trying to make themselves sound smart. Little words were just fine and didn't have ya looking like a dickweed.

See? I could use big words too!

I slid off the hospital bed, tiptoed from behind the curtain, and rushed out the door before anyone even realized I was missing. The halls over here were just as empty but I could feel the cameras watching me, so I looked up and gave them a little wave. They didn't wave back, though. They never did.

I continued skipping down the hall until I found the locker room where all the doctors and nurses and *murses* liked to clean up and get changed. They didn't like having blood on them. I didn't mind it so much. I kinda like the sticky feel when it was almost dried.

A murse had taken me into this locker room before, said it was more private than the bays. And he was right. I let him come all over my face and he gave me an M&M bag full of colorful pills and a joint.

I missed that part the most, being able to fuck and smoke whenever I wanted. Here I had to wait until one of the guards could sneak off. Then again, I did like it when they didn't know I knew they were watching me touch myself through that little glass window on my door. They would touch themselves too. I enjoyed that part more. It was like watching the cap of a soda pop blow off when ya shook it too hard.

I shook my head, finally remembering why I was here, and tugged on each of the locker room doors until one of them opened and I found a pair of leggings and an old t-shirt. I took off my itchy hospital clothes and shoved them into the locker.

"Tradesies!" I giggled to myself before tugging the leggings up my legs and throwing the shirt over my head. Then I snooped around until I found a pair of shoes that fit. A few squirts of perfume and a comb through my hair and I was finally looking like my old self.

Pressing a hand to the locker room door, I popped my head out into the hallway, my mop of red hair brushing against the floor before my feet followed it.

All the alarms were going off now and I could hear sirens in the background. That meant that whoever was being *emergencied* was super important. Funny enough, the super important guys always had the smallest dicks. I could tell ya from experience.

I skipped back past the medical ward and out the back door, looking for someone to play with, but there was no one out here either. Just a big ol' truck-van thing. I tugged the driver's door open and found a set of keys inside.

Finders keepers!

I adjusted the seat and the mirrors like my daddy taught me and glanced up at the reflection of my green eyes staring back at me.

"Okay, Nickie Saint James, I think it's time we blow this popsicle stand. What do ya say? You in or are you out?"

CHAPTER 31
RUDY

ucking nutjob. Fuck you, Nickie. Fuck you, Prat.

"We haven't been out this way because of the storm. Maybe we can find some more…" My words trailed off as I realized… I was alone. "Fuck you, Quentin."

That one hurt. Out of anyone, I didn't think that I'd lose Que, but here I was, walking in the goddamn dark by my-fucking-self.

What was fucking new? I'd always been the only one to actually do anything worth a damn in our mismatched group of fuckups. There was a reason I was the designated leader. I was the biggest fuck up of them all.

I thought about the guys. About Vix and how bad his drinking had become since we'd escaped. The asshole had sobered up in prison, as much as he was able to while avoiding all the readily available contraband. He'd gotten his dumbass put there in the first place for beating the shit out of his boss for taking a liquor bottle away from him. You'd think that would have been enough to keep him off the stuff.

Clearly it wasn't.

The twins, Donnor and Connor, were fucking computer geniuses, who lacked any real-world smarts. Sometimes I wondered how they hadn't landed themselves on the other side of the building, the one the state had sectioned off into an asylum with all the looners. I mean, you had to be fucking crazy to think you'd get away with hacking into multiple government databases and then bragging about it to all your cyber pals.

Dane was probably the most innocent of us. His shit was a pure stroke of bad luck. Sure, he'd killed someone, same as I did. But it had been accidental. He'd hit a patch of black ice, spun out, and plowed into some rich guy's kid. I think that, that was what made him so angry all the time. He was just a regular dude, and now he would always be remembered as a criminal. A killer.

Fuck, come to think of it, every time he looked in the mirror that gnarly scar served as a reminder that there was no real escaping anything for him...

Then you had Blitz. Bad drug deal and a rivalry gone wrong. Nothing all that complex, but at his core, Blitz was caring, funny, easygoing, and a good fucking friend.

As for Dash, he would be crucified for the hand he played in all this. He was the reason any of us had a fucking chance at being normal again. I never did see him as a nurse. He hated most of the assholes he worked with, the patients too. Until he met Que for the first time. And then his thinking changed. Guy became our biggest advocate after that.

And Que? Well, the fucker signed his life away when he convinced me Holly wasn't worth mine. He hadn't even questioned it. What would happen to him or me. Or both of us if—*when* we were caught. He'd simply said: *You've punished yourself enough. Let me help you. I got you. You know I've always been here for you, Rudolph.*

I didn't know what Prat did. He never told any of us, and honestly no one cared or judged him. He barely spoke, mostly just grunted in your direction, but the man was massive with more muscles than any of us combined. That's what made this so hard. I couldn't read him like the others.

Did he get away? Or did something far worse happen to him? What was I missing?

I shook my head. What was I even doing out here? I needed to grab Nickie by her hair and drag her out to that damn lake and demand to know why those keys were under the floorboard. Why they were covered in someone's blood.

"Fuck you!" I screamed to no one and nothing but flurries of snow. Then I dropped to my knees, the weight of this shit feeling as heavy as the shackles I'd been trying to escape.

Freedom. That was all we wanted. A chance to live out our lives just like everyone else. None of us had been perfect, but I didn't think we deserved tossing away either.

We'd found solace in one another. A family. I loved every single one of those assholes. I'd die for them. The shivers racked my spine, and I realized that just might happen if I didn't turn my ass around and go back to the cabin.

Maybe Que talked to Nickie. Maybe it was all a misunderstanding of some sort. Maybe Prat had driven the van into the lake on purpose. Maybe he'd been followed and needed to ditch it. Maybe he'd gotten injured and hidden that key there for us to find...

Fuck! Nothing was making fucking sense!

"Where the fuck are you, Prat!"

The blaring light of the prison spotters and sniper towers climbed over the tree line, and I sighed. Maybe this was a sign that I should just turn myself in. Make up some lie about everyone else being dead and give them a real chance at freedom.

"I'm sorry, Que," I said and headed that way.

THE CLOSER I GOT TO THE PRISON, THE DEEPER THE chill cut through to my bones. I could already feel the hounds snapping at my heels, smell their foul breath on my face. I was going to die out here before I—

"Oof!" Something caught on my boot, and I tripped, landing face-first in the snow. I sat up and growled before getting back to my feet and kicking at the lump in anger. "The fuck!"

The lump... moved. I froze before brushing aside my shock and crouching down to see what it was. I dusted off the collection of snow and jumped back again when I found a pair of dead eyes staring at me.

It was a body. Not just a body. But...

"Prat."

My friend's face was frozen in the snow, *frozen in terror,* bits of blood and skin peeling away as I scraped some of the ice off. This didn't look like the work of any animal I'd ever seen. Animals also didn't leave their meals behind. And there were no bullet wounds suggesting someone in the tower had spotted him. So what the fuck had happened?

"Oh god. Prat," I repeated aloud. "What the fuck happened to you?"

He still had Dash's old scrubs on, but the bottoms were yanked down, exposing him to the dick. People didn't just yank their dicks out when they were dying. It wasn't normal...

And neither was someone else. Fucking Nickie. She'd done this. I didn't know how I knew. I just did. It was a gut feeling, like the ones I used to get when I knew a perp was lying to me. I was never wrong then, and I wasn't wrong now either.

She would answer for this. She would...

"Fuck! Que!" My throat felt like it was closing up. He was at the cabin. With her. They all were. "Fuck! No, no, no!" I pushed up on shaky legs and took off in a full sprint, trying to follow my boot prints back to him while the snow did its best to cover them up.

I couldn't lose Que. I couldn't. He was the one good thing in my fucking life. If Nickie touched any of them I'd kill her, but if she hurt *him*, I'd become the monster the outside world deemed me to be.

"Que!" I yelled, blinded by frozen tears as I pounded snow. I never cried. Not even for Holly. Because Que wasn't her. He was different. He was... Fuck, he was everything. "I... I love you, you fucking idiot! You better be okay!"

Love? What the fuck was I saying?

The truth. Because I did love him. It had just taken me this long to figure it out. It made about as much sense as it didn't. Holly had been the rational choice. A check box. The way my life was supposed to turn out. I'd been a cop and she'd been a teacher. They fit together like peanut butter and jelly.

But I fucking hated peanut butter. I loved things that weren't good for me. Like marshmallow fluff. And Twinkie cakes and Cool Whip... And Quentin. I loved him.

And now he was in trouble because I didn't trust my gut the first time I felt something was off with that girl.

I ran faster, and faster still, my legs burning as hot as the pain in my chest until it was replaced by something cold.

THWACK!

"Ow! What the fuck?" I shook my head and tried to regain my bearings. Did something hit me or did I hit it?

"Slow the fuck down!" A familiar voice huffed and heaved. "Not all of us have bionic legs!"

I spun around, terrified that I was imagining shit. Hearing what I wanted to hear. Then my eyes landed on him and I tackled the man like a linebacker, slamming him down onto the snow and rolling on top of him. Forcing him to drop the hand-sized ball of ice he was preparing to chuck at me again.

"Oh my god! Que! You're okay! You're really okay! I thought... I thought I lost you. I thought..."

"Well, you kinda did." He grinned up at me. "You need to learn not to walk so fast. I almost fucked like six different trees thinking they were you."

"Almost?" I laughed, as a sense of giddiness took over.

"You can pluck the splinters out of my dick later." Que shrugged, then pushed me back to study my eyes. "What's going on, Rudolph?"

I wiped at my face, trying to recover from the emotional whiplash. "I can't lose you, Quentin Laurent. Ever. Like fucking ever. I fucking love you. I'm sorry it took me so long to admit that to myself—but I see it now. I get it now. It's always been you and me. I fucking love you, Thumper."

"'Bout time, ice king," he grumbled, but I could see the tears forming in his eyes too. "The thing is... it never really mattered. Because you've always been mine. I was just waitin' for you to know I was yours too."

I nodded, unable to find the words to express my relief. The rightness and completion. So, instead, I grabbed his beautifully stupid, perfect face and kissed him. Pulling back to add, "Fuck me."

Que chuckled, stopping when he realized I was serious.

I rolled my jumpsuit and underwear down under my ass and started for his next.

"Oh, fuck! Okay... Are you sure? You want your first time to be... out here? In the dirt?"

"As opposed to a prison cell like *you* wanted?" I laughed. After the food fight that brought us together, I should have known the guy was a romantic.

Before Que could argue with me, I slid down his body, pressed myself between his thighs, grabbed his cock, and popped it into my mouth. It didn't take him long to get filthy and wet—hell, the fucker was so worked up he nearly came down my throat.

I popped off him and climbed back up. Watching as he swished his saliva around his cheeks before hocking it onto his fingers. Then he tugged me closer for a kiss, fucking my mouth with his tongue in time with the way his hand was fucking my ass.

This was as far as it ever went before. The one line I wouldn't cross. I couldn't explain the logic to anyone who wasn't in my head. Why fucking a dude felt slightly less wrong than letting him fuck me. Or maybe it never had anything to do with wrong or right. Maybe it was because I knew that once I let him have that part of me, there was no turning back. There was no me without him. Even though that had always been the case anyway.

Once he felt I was good and ready, Que rolled us over. Gave his dick another glob of spit and pressed it against my ass. Pushing inside me at an excruciatingly slow pace.

"Hurry up and fuck me. I need to feel your come inside me. All of it. Don't let a fucking drop escape, you understand?" I grunted, ignoring the burn and embracing the pleasure.

"Can't help but top from the bottom, can ya, baby?" Que laughed before slamming all the way forward.

I didn't have time to unpack that, because he was already *thumping* into me. Breaking my brain and my asshole. "Ah, fuck. Yes... Make me a bottom then. Show me why you should be the one in charge."

Que met my challenge, dominating my asshole, my mouth, any part of me he could reach and touch and suck until I was spraying come all over his chest and abs. "Just like that, baby. You're so beautiful when you come for me. Take it. Take this dick. Make it yours."

And I did. I relaxed for once in my fucking life, laid back, and let go.

"Fuck yes! I'm coming! You feel so fucking good, baby.

So fucking perfect," Que grunted, his body spasming, and his smile wider than I'd ever seen it before. And I knew it was worth it. Giving this to him. Giving myself to him the way he had given himself to me a long time ago.

I even allowed myself to bask in the glow for a minute, reaching up a hand to brush the blonde hair from those bright-blue doe eyes. Dropping my arm back to my side as soon as I spotted the dried blood on my fingertips.

"Hey, what's wrong?" Que asked, immediately recognizing the shift in me.

I rolled him off my chest, tugged my clothes back into place, and jumped to my feet. Then I started pacing while digging a little one-sided path in the snow.

I didn't even know how to explain it. So I didn't.

"Prat's dead," I blurted out, my body racked with shivers that had nothing to do with the cold.

Que grabbed my hands and met my eyes. I didn't remember him getting up. "What do you mean he's dead?"

I swallowed the lump in my throat. "That's why I was running. He's dead. He was killed. I was trying to get to you. To make sure she didn't—" I knew I sounded crazy but if anyone would listen to what I had to say, crazy or not, it was this man in front of me. "And I think Nickie was the one who killed him."

CHAPTER 32
PRAT

reedom. My God... I gestured the sign of the cross over my chest. *We were actually free.*

The gurgling in my stomach was making me weak in my knees, but I had to push through this for the guys. They were counting on me. I just had to get to the van Dash left idling by the back door and wait for them. Then we would all head to the cabin to regroup. It was our final checkpoint before hitting the road. If we got separated, we'd all agreed to meet there. Plan was to switch out vehicles at random spots along the way, use cash, and stay under the radar. No big moves, no drama.

And for the first time, I felt it in my soul. This could actually work.

I was racing through the halls in Dash's scrubs when all of a sudden the lights flashed and the sirens began to blare in my ears.

Darn it! Did they catch Dash? The others?

I couldn't think like that. I had to keep running. My heart rate picking up the moment the exit sign came into view. I pushed out the unlocked double doors just like in all our trial runs, and spotted the van right where he'd said it'd be. That final rush of adrenaline hit my veins and I sprinted forward, only to skid to a stop when our designated getaway car backed up and sped off.

Something was wrong. *Why were they leaving without me?*

I glanced down at the watch Dash had sneaked into my cell. I was right on time. It didn't make sense.

"Wait!" I hollered, taking off after the van, my shoes kicking up gravel as I bolted down the prison driveway and out the employee gates. "Stop! Guys! It's me!"

They weren't stopping. If anything, they were speeding up and I was falling behind. My chest heaved as I tried to remember the layout of the woods from the prior runs. I knew what I was doing. I'd done it before. I just wasn't thinking straight.

I told myself they must have been heading for the cabin, and I knew exactly where that was. How to get there in the dark and do it quietly. I thought Rudy was being overcautious when he kept insisting we play it out again. And again. And again. Now, I was glad he did.

So instead of worrying about where the van was going, I focused on making my way to the cabin. Not stopping until I could see the smoke billowing out of the old chimney. That was a good sign, right? That meant someone had started a fire. Someone was in there. It'd had always looked abandoned before.

I glanced around. I didn't see the van, but that didn't mean they weren't smart enough to stash it somewhere.

I slid down the little snow-covered hill on the heels of my boots, waiting until I was steady on my feet, and approached the door. Clearing my throat, lifting my arm, and finally mustering the courage to knock. A few moments later, the door creaked open and a little old lady about half my height appeared on the other side.

Oh no...

I looked down at her but she didn't seem inclined to look up at me. Instead, she smiled and started fussing with my scrubs. "Oh, hello!"

"Uh... hi?" I replied, trying out the voice I'd heard Que use on anything that walked over the years. A mix between soft, sweet, and sultry.

"You came to see me?" she asked, her glassy eyes finally drawing up towards my face. But it was clear she couldn't *see me.*

Was she blind?

"Daryl? That's you, right, dear?"

I swallowed, feeling the chill eat my ass and hell's gates open up behind me from what I was about to do. "Yeah... it's me."

THE MORE COOKIES THIS OLD LADY SHOVED INTO MY face, the more my stomach soured with the guilt. She kept going on and on about how much she'd missed me, how she hadn't seen any of her other grandbabies since the death of their parents. This woman had no one. And here I was, pretending to be some long-lost *dirtbag* grandson, who didn't have enough time in his day to come out and check on his elderly grandmother.

Guess he and I had that in common. We were both dirtbags now.

Gertrude never stopped knitting, her hands moving of their own accord while she chatted away. Almost as if she could sense me watching her, she smiled. "The devil's lettuce."

My head shot up to look at her. "Hm?"

"It's good for these old hands, helps with the pain."

"Right," I replied before mindlessly plopping another cookie into my mouth.

"Oh, you sure can eat, dearie. Just like when you were little. Do you remember? I still make your favorites every Christmas weekend just in case you happen to stop by."

"Yeah... Gran. I sure do love 'em. And, uh, the others do too. They'll be here soon, ya know? We all came back to spend the holidays with you."

Hell. That's where I was going. The cross swinging around her neck was like a metronome counting my sins, damning me the longer I sat here and fed her lies while she fed me cookies.

I kept glancing out the frosted window, waiting for the rest of the guys to appear. Praying no one got caught up and realizing how ironic that was. No one was listening to my prayers anymore. Not after this.

At least we'd be safe, get a warm meal and maybe some rest. Gertrude was a decent human being. Hopefully life treated her well when we went on our way in the morning. I'd be sure to send her a card next Christmas or maybe some flowers or something since I wasn't sure how much she could see. I'd even sign it off *from Daryl.*

If I was gonna make myself out to be a liar, I might as well spare an old woman some heartache while I was at it.

The cuckoo clock kept ticking behind me, and I couldn't help but stare at the picture of Gertrude hanging on the wall. Just her, no family in sight. They'd all abandoned her in some way, and here we were about to do the same thing. Use her for her kindness and ditch her.

Convicts indeed.

Never in my life did I feel more like a monster than in this moment. Not even after I turned myself in for murdering my wife. It was a mortal sin, ya know. The kind that didn't come with forgiveness. No amount of "Hail Marys" or "Our Fathers" could save this damned soul of mine.

But Margie had been sick. Suffering, and the doctors had refused to give her any sort of relief. She'd begged me just to let her sleep. Suicide was another mortal sin. So, I'd had a choice to make, my soul or hers. The answer was simple. My wife had been a good woman, far better than me. She deserved to go to heaven. If that made me a villain for giving her the morphine that ended her suffering and took her life, so be it.

I glanced down at my watch, even though I could still hear the clock ticking from the living room. I was starting to get anxious. Maybe the guys couldn't find the cabin. They hadn't even been headed in the right direction when they made a left instead of a right after turning out of the gates.

I sighed and wiped my mouth with the napkin Gertrude gave me. "Uh, Gran, I'm gonna go check on the others, make sure they didn't get lost."

"Of course, dearie! I'll have a plate ready for you all when you return."

As soon as I stepped outside the door, the cold air slapping me in the face, I took a deep breath and made my way back towards the prison. The storm was picking up, and the chill traveled through my pants and scrub top, while the surgical cap on my head was too porous to protect my bald head from anything.

That was it! They probably got turned around in the blizzard. It was one thing we didn't discuss in detail. What to do if the roads were blocked.

I followed the tracks until the silhouette of the van appeared in the distance. Parked in plain sight, while the fumes puffed out of the exhaust like these dummies were trying to get caught.

Shaking my head, I jogged out in front of them, waving my arms and calling out, "Guys! It's okay! The cabin's just down her—"

My words were cut off as the van pulled back onto the road and headed in my direction. I skidded to a stop and watched as the high beams flashed across my face.

They were driving too fast. Closer and closer, the engine revving, and the uneven terrain causing the rusted shocks to bounce the cab around.

"What the fuck?" I waved my arms again but they weren't slowing down. "Hey!" I shouted, diving out of the way before they plowed me over. I rolled across the road and landed on my back in a pile of snow. "Guys! Stop! It's me, Prat!" I called out again.

But they couldn't hear me and they didn't stop. Instead, they were backing up and launching forward. This time I had no chance to get out of the way, and I screamed as the tires cracked my ribs and mangled my legs. I couldn't move. I was paralyzed, unable to do anything but stare up at the night sky, the twinkling stars, and the blinding headlights.

They... hit me...

I heard the driver's side door open and tried to crane my neck to get a better look. But all I could see was a woman. Red hair the color of the fires of hell dangling over me. She tilted her head, sliding a finger down my broken body and across my borrowed scrubs.

"Sorry, Doc. But I will not go back there," she whispered, her voice sounding both sad and amused.

"Please... don't..." I choked out.

"Aw, what's that I hear? You wanna play, huh?" She sighed, tugging on my scrub bottoms and using her cold hands to stroke me hard. I hadn't let another woman touch me since my wife. And that's when the truth landed like a punch to my gut...

This was hell. That's what this was. I'd died and gone to hell.

It was the only way my brain could process what was happening, my body numb to the cold. To the heat between her thighs as she mounted me. To the pain in what was left of my legs. I couldn't fight her. I couldn't breathe, the fire in my lungs drowning me as sure as the flames in the pits of hell.

I'm sorry, guys.

"Shhh. Go to sleep, Doc. Everything will be okay."

I'm sorry, Margie.

With a stuttering breath, I closed my eyes. And my last thought was that, in the end, there was no freedom for me.

I'd died a prisoner.

CHAPTER 33
NICKIE

I walked over to Gran's dresser and patted the scrub cap I'd placed there shortly after I'd arrived on her doorstep. That man on the road had been so pretty. Like the rocking horse my daddy got me when I was five. I liked to ride that almost as much.

It was a shame I had to leave him out in the snow for the wolves. He was the reason I'd found Granny after all. His boot tracks had led me right to her. Otherwise I would have been lost in those woods. Running around, covered in his blood, with nowhere to go.

I sighed, stroking the bloody cap and letting the fond memory float around my brain and make my insides tingle.

"Mmm," I moaned, jumping up on the bed and trailing my hands down to my dripping cunt. The boys were all asleep—except Rabbit Man and Soda Pop, who were still holed up in Granny's knitting room. Maybe they'd come find me when they were finished...

I started to make slow circles around my clit, but then a fly flew around my face and I gagged when one almost sneaked up my nose.

"Ick! Really, Gran?" I looked over at where she was resting on a pillow and swiped at the bugs buzzing around her open mouth.

"Shoo. Go *bug* someone else. Gran's sleeping," I scolded them and tucked the covers up over her neck a little tighter. "There you go."

I gave her forehead a kiss, mindful of the knitting needle sticking out of her eyeball. Granny always did love to knit.

That was the problem, I suppose. She'd made it too easy. At least sissy had screamed. Gran just stared through me like she couldn't see me until, well, she really couldn't.

"Night, night, Gran. I have my boys to tend to. They're good boys, aren't they? You'd like them. I think I'll keep them."

And I meant it. I did like my boys. They each had their own quirks, and I enjoyed making them laugh and smile. And come. I enjoyed *that last one* the most. All of them except Doc. He was sleeping like Gran.

I'd never say it out loud but I was glad Dash wasn't a doc. I'd hate to have to run him over too. Murses were much better. Murses patched you up and gave you candy. Docs were the ones always trying to get you to do stuff you didn't want to do. Like take your meds and listen to their orders.

"Think I should keep them, Granny?" I asked, hopping to my feet and adjusting my picture to better fit in her frame.

It was my favorite. Given to me by my daddy the last

time he'd come to visit. I'd kept it in my bra, along with the one he'd given me the time before that. I had to be careful with the scissors and glue but Gran and I looked good together. Much better than me and Sissy. We were a family now. A home.

A pair of shadows caught my eye from where they danced across the frosted window, and I rushed over and held a hand to the glass, rubbing away at the fog until I could see them more clearly. Soda Pop and Rabbit Man were headed this way. Those sneaky links musta crept out the door without me knowing.

But they were coming back for me. Just like I said they would.

Grabbing another old dress from Granny's closet, I swiped it over my head and adjusted my boobies in the vanity mirror. Then, giving Gran one last look, I flipped off the light and waved before shutting the door and locking it back up to keep the bugs inside and away from my boys.

Nothing would hurt them now. They were mine.

I skipped towards the front door with a giggle, gripped the knob, and twisted. Eager to greet them. It was Christmas morning and Santa had brought me the best gift of all. Someone to play with.

Sure, nine *someones* crammed together in a tiny cabin in the middle of the woods might not have been ideal, but like Granny always said, when it came to family... the more, the merrier.

THE END

ACKNOWLEDGMENTS

THANKS TO EVERYONE WHO HAS BEEN A PART OF THIS LONG-ASS PROCESS. TO EVERYONE WHO HAS SHARED, LIKED, COMMENTED, AND PREORDERED. TO THOSE OF YOU WHO TOOK A CHANCE ON US AND OUR FUCKED-UP BRAINS. AND TO THOSE WHO LOVE THE FICTIONAL CHARACTERS THAT LIVE RENT FREE IN OUR HEADS. WE COULD NOT HAVE DONE IT WITHOUT YOU, AND WE ARE SO VERY HUMBLED.

WE ALSO WANTED TO SAY THANK YOU TO OUR ARC READERS, WHO ARE TAKING TIME OUT OF THEIR BUSY SCHEDULES TO READ AND REVIEW OUR BOOK. AND THANK YOU TO THOSE OF YOU WHO WENT AS FAR AS TO READ AND REVIEW OUR PRIOR PUBLICATIONS TOO—"WE SEE YOU" AND WE ARE SO GRATEFUL FOR YOU.

ALSO BY SYBIL KNIGHT

THE TRUTH AND LIES DUET:

The Harsher the Truth

The Sweeter the Lies

THE RENEGADES SERIES:

Skin

Lamb

Bells

STANDALONE NOVELS:

Half Cocked

Kill Joy

STANDALONES:

LITTLE AUTHOR

BORROWED

BLOODY VALENTINE

BODY TOX

MARA

HIS TRICK

JINX

MORE TITLES TO COME...

ABOUT THE AUTHOR
SYBIL KNIGHT

SYBIL IS A TRUE EAST COASTER WITH A LOVE FOR TRUE CRIME AND CAFFEINE. WHEN SHE ISN'T WORKING OR WRITING, SHE IS TALKING ABOUT WORKING OR WRITING.

HER STORIES RANGE FROM GRAY TO BLACK, WITH DARKER THEMES THROUGHOUT. SHE PREFERS HEROINES WITH A KICK-ASS MENTALITY AND THE HEROES WHO KNOW HOW TO REIN THEM IN. THE MENTAL AND MEDICAL ASPECTS OF HER BOOKS ARE WELL-RESEARCHED, THOUGH THEY ARE GIVEN A HUMANISTIC APPROACH AND DIAGNOSES AREN'T THE FOCAL POINTS. SHE BELIEVES HER CHARACTERS DON'T NEED TO WEAR LABELS IN ORDER TO GET THEIR MESSAGES ACROSS.

HER BOOKS ARE MOSTLY STANDALONES, THOUGH HER CHARACTERS MAY INTERACT AND INTERSECT WORLDS. ADDITIONALLY, SHE WORKS CLOSELY WITH AND WRITES ALONGSIDE AUTHOR DAHLIA REIGN AND SOME CHARACTERS WILL APPEAR IN CAMEOS IN EACH OF THEIR PUBLICATIONS.

SYBIL WELCOMES EMAILS FROM READERS IF THERE ARE CONCERNS OR QUESTIONS REGARDING ANY OF HER PUBLICATIONS.

EMAIL: **AUTHORSYBILKNIGHT@GMAIL.COM**

ABOUT THE AUTHOR
SK PRYNTZ

SK Pryntz loves writing gritty, thrilling, dark tales that will twist you into knots until you can't stand it. Her love of writing began at an early age, as well as singing and reading about fairy tales. However, as she has grown older, the real versions of fairy tales are sincerely her favorites.

When she surfaces from her writing caves, she loves spending time with her husband and children.

HTTPS://LINKTR.EE/SKPRYNTZAUTHOR